Other Romance Stories by R.W. Wallace

French Office Romance Series
Flirting in Plain Sight
Hiding in Plain Sight
Loving in Plain Sight

Holiday Short Stories
Down the Memory Aisle

Love at First Flight
by R.W. Wallace

Copyright © 2022 by R.W. Wallace

Copy editing by Wendy Janes
Cover by R.W. Wallace
Cover Illustration 8427280 © baavli | Depositphotos
Cover Illustration 139991546 © VitalyGrin | Depositphotos

All characters and events in this book, other than those clearly in the public domain, are fictitious and any resemblance to real persons, living or dead, is purely coincidental.

All rights reserved. No part of this publication may be reproduced, distributed, or transmitted in any form or by any means, including photocopying, recording, or other electronic or mechanical methods, without the prior written permission of the publisher, except in the case of brief quotations embodied in critical reviews and certain other noncommercial uses permitted by copyright law.

www.rwwallace.com

ISBN paperback: [978-2-493670-05-2]
ISBN ebook: [978-2-493670-06-9]

First Edition

FROM THE AUTHOR OF FLIRTING IN PLAIN SIGHT

R.W. WALLACE

Love at First Flight

A Sweet Romance

To Beth

*for reading and loving the story
despite it being a dreaded romance*

ONE

Next Level Torture

Thomas

THE FIST COMES out of nowhere.

I've been stuck in my seat by the window since take-off, watching the sun rise over an infinite sea of white, bumpy clouds, keeping myself occupied by trying to figure out which countries and which cities we're flying over, based only on the duration of the flight and the rare glimpses of the Earth below us. I'm *pretty* sure we're over northern France now but it's impossible to tell for sure since I can't see any major mountain ranges, lakes, or easily recognizable cities.

My connection in Schiphol was a short one and I had to sprint from Terminal A to Terminal C in ten minutes in order to catch my flight. I think I knocked over one elderly lady on my way off one of the moving walkways, one mother cursed me to hell and back for "making" her five-year-old run after me when she'd probably told him repeatedly that no, you're not allowed to run inside the terminal, and I gave about a hundred people an excellent anecdote to tell their friends at home when I tripped over my own feet in front of a burger place and almost lost a knee cap when I landed on my own carry-on luggage.

I'm one hundred percent certain my suitcase isn't in the cargo hold below me. It's probably getting a guided tour of the Amsterdam airport and will join me in Toulouse in a day or two.

My main issue right now, though, is that I didn't have the time to visit the men's room before boarding my flight. I figured it wasn't a big deal; I just had to hold out until we were in the air, and I could use the restroom in the aircraft.

Except my neighbor, a pretty lady in her mid-thirties who boarded with a carry-on that shouldn't be allowed to qualify as a handbag but probably does in her eyes and two duty-free shopping bags clearly filled to the brim with chocolate and sweets, sat down with a huge sigh of relief when she arrived—and proceeded to fall asleep before we'd even left the gate.

She didn't wake up on take-off, she didn't react to the no smoking sign being switched off, she didn't hear the hostesses coming past with their trolley of tasteless sandwiches and drinks, and she didn't move a muscle when a baby three rows back screamed its head off for five minutes straight. Her hands stayed immobile in her lap, her head stayed glued to the headrest with her neck bent back at a painful angle, and her mouth stayed open in a position that student me would have seen as an open invitation to do something stupid if it had been one of my friends.

Now we're thirty minutes out of Toulouse, which isn't very long, all things considered, but I just can't take it anymore. I'm wondering how much a bladder can take before it bursts and does permanent damage. This is some next level torture.

Love at First Flight

I attempted to move around a little in my seat some time ago, hoping the woman would wake up and see that I needed to get past her, but no luck.

I think we could crash and she wouldn't wake up.

I considered the possibility of trying to step over her to get out but we're flying coach and I'm fairly certain the space between the woman's gaping mouth and the seat in front of her is smaller than the width of my hips. I don't want to test it, either, because if I *am* too big, I'll be rubbing either my ass or my crotch against the poor woman's face.

When my teeth start tingling and I start shivering, I give up. I won't be able to wait another thirty minutes until we land and then *another* fifteen to twenty before getting out of the airplane.

So I decide to wake my neighbor. She'll have to wake up soon to get off, anyway, right?

I gently place on hand on her shoulder. Get out, "Excuse me, Madame, but—"

She clocks me in the face.

My head snaps back. My glasses fall off and into my lap.

At first, the pain doesn't even register. It's just shock. She *hit* me! Not merely a slap, either, but a proper right hook aimed perfectly for my left eye.

"What the—" One hand goes to my face. The other picks up my glasses.

The lenses aren't broken but the frame is bent completely out of shape. The left branch is no longer attached at a ninety degree angle but something closer to a one-eighty. She *flattened* them against my face.

That's when I register the pain. The one spot on the side of my nose where the pad was pretty much embedded into my skin. My cheekbone is on fire—I think the frames connected with the bone. And a quick touch to my brow confirms that I'm bleeding—the glasses must have cut into my skin.

The glasses protected my eyes but made significant damage to the area around them.

Note to self: don't get hit in the face while wearing glasses.

As the shock starts to wear off, my original pressing matter reminds me why I woke the woman in the first place.

"Let me out," I say, my voice harsh and urgent. I no longer care about politeness and niceties and what others might think. I need to use the bathroom, I need to see a mirror, and I need to be alone for a minute or two so my mind can wrap itself around what just happened.

I push on the woman's shoulder again. "I need to use the restroom. Let me out. Or I'm stepping over you."

Eyes wide, she scrambles to unfasten her seatbelt and jumps out of her seat.

I rush past her, run down the aisle toward the back of the plane while keeping my eyes on my destination and stubbornly not seeing the upturned faces of the other passengers. I ignore the surprised expressions on the faces of the two hostesses chatting in the back, tear open the lavatory door, and cram myself into the tiny space.

What the hell just happened?

TWO

I Wasn't Supposed to Turn to the Dark Side

Isabelle

I JUST PUNCHED a guy in the face. He woke me up from a sleep so deep I'd lost all track of time and place, and *I hit him*.

As he rushes into the lavatory at the back of the plane, all the other passengers staring at him in shock, I stand in the aisle, one hand on the seat of the guy in front of me for balance, my heart thumping loudly in my ears, and my brain still not up and running.

Before getting on this flight, I hadn't slept for thirty hours. When my brain was finally allowed to switch off, it really switched off.

I'm trying to reboot but I'm stuck in a loop of *I hit him, I hit him*. My breath is short, like I've run a marathon. I'm not sure I can feel my hands.

I don't know how to manage this on top of everything else. I've never been in the position of the bad guy before. I'm always the victim. I'm *used* to being the victim. Not the bully.

It took me years to work up the guts to leave, to do what was best for *me*, saying stop to the crap that everybody kept throwing my way. But I wasn't supposed to turn to the dark side.

One of the flight hostesses, a tall blonde woman with green eye-shadow and blood-red lipstick, comes up behind me. "Is there a problem, Madame?"

"She just punched her neighbor in the face," a lady in her fifties who's sitting on the row behind mine says helpfully. "I saw everything. He only tried to talk to her and she punched him. His glasses are broken."

I don't even know how to feel or react. Normally, I'd take exception to someone using that tone talking about me—because I never do anything wrong. There's never a reason to talk to me like that, so if someone tries it, it's unjustified and I'll…get upset. I wish I could say I let them know they're wrong and put them in their place, but I can never come up with a clever comeback in time. Or get my voice to work correctly.

But I'll be raging on the inside because the mean things they said about me are wrong.

This woman isn't wrong.

I look to the back of the plane, but the man is still in the lavatory. I hope he isn't too badly hurt.

"Madame," the hostess says, her voice much cooler than a moment ago, "Would you please accompany me to the back of the plane?"

As I nod numbly and walk down the aisle, dozens of curious eyes tracking my movement, I try to remember what the appropriate behavior would be in this situation. What are you supposed to do when you hit someone by accident? Maybe if I'd been more violent in my youth, I would have known the answer to that question?

I reach the storage area at the back before my mind can come up with any more ridiculous ideas.

The two other hostesses are already there, meaning I now have all three of them looking at me. Identical uniforms, different makeup, same cool expressions.

"Madame, would you mind telling us what just happened?" the blonde one says. "Did you hit another passenger?"

"Is that what happened?" the hostess with a black pixie cut says. "You hit the man who's in the lavatory right now? The one with blood running down his chin?"

My hands fly to my face as I gasp. "He was *bleeding*? Oh my God, I have to go apologize."

I rush to the lavatory door and try to open it. It's locked, of course. So I knock. And then pound on it.

"Madame!" The blonde one grabs my hands to get me to stop. "You are not helping your case by being violent."

"I'm not being violent! I want to apologize. I *never* hit people. Ever! I have to apologize and make sure he's okay." I start pounding on the lavatory door with my other hand.

The hostess grabs that one too. "You can apologize when we land. Right now, you need to return to your seat and stay there until everybody else has deplaned."

Oh God, they're going to call the police on me.

There's no reason to think Pierre has reported me missing to the police yet. I'm not missing, I've barely been gone a day. And even if he did go to the police, it would be the English one, not the French.

Interpol won't come after you for walking out on your husband, right?

The confusion of waking up so abruptly has cleared, finally. But my mess of a life is back and I don't like it. My hands still blocked by the blonde hostess, I let my head bang into the lavatory door.

As a way of knocking? An expression of my frustration? Who knows. I certainly don't.

The lock clicks and the door opens.

THREE

I'm Never Going to Hear the End of This

Thomas

BEING FINALLY ALLOWED to relieve myself is almost orgasmic. My teeth tingle, goosebumps break out all over my body, and I have to bite my fist to keep from moaning out loud.

Once that's taken care of, I turn to the mirror.

She certainly knows how to throw a punch. My nose is sore and there's still a slight indentation where the pad was shoved into my skin. My cheekbone is painful and as I poke at the skin below my eye, I can feel my cheek already swelling. That's going to become one hell of a shiner by tomorrow. I'll have to ask the flight attendants if they have any ice.

The cut on my brow is tiny. So small, in fact, that it has already stopped bleeding. It doesn't make the streak of blood down the left side of my face any less impressive.

I grab a tissue from a dispenser on the wall and wipe away the blood. Then I take three more, soak them in tepid water from the sink, and place them on my cheek. It probably won't make much of a difference but it helps to *do* something.

The visual of my friend Vincent picking me up at the airport, seeing the shiner, and learning a girl punched me because I needed to pee appears in my mind, and I burst out laughing. I'm never going to hear the end of this.

Someone knocks at the door and I jump and drop the wet tissues to the floor. I don't bother to try to pick them up—this place is so cramped, I'm not certain I can bend down without knocking into a wall.

The knocking turns into pounding. I hear voices but not what they're saying because of the roar of the engines.

I really wouldn't mind staying in here alone and isolated until the plane lands. I don't want people to stare, and I'd prefer to lick my wounds in peace. But it might be someone who's as pressed as I was to use the lavatory, or the flight attendants wanting me back in my seat for landing.

Taking a deep breath, I grab my broken glasses from the sink. I think I hear another thud, and I slide the lock open and open the door.

The thing about airplane lavatory doors, though, is that since there's so little space, they don't open in or out, but rather fold in on themselves toward the inside of the lavatory. So if someone is, say, leaning face-first against the door on the outside, once the door is unlocked, said person will find themselves falling into the room, and into the door itself.

I barely have time to register a head of messy black hair and the faces of three surprised flight attendants before I receive a weight in the chest and am pushed to the back of the lavatory, my knees hitting the toilet bowl and the rest of me hovering over it until my back hits the wall.

"Oh my God, I'm so sorry." The black hair is in my face now, some rosy scent tickling my nose. Hands are pushing against my chest, using me as a support to get back up.

"Madame, you need to—" A blonde flight attendant appears in the open doorway.

"Oh, no, you don't! I need to apologize, is what I need. You just—" A grunt. The door closes and I hear the lock slide back in place.

I'm sitting on the toilet bowl now, deciding these pants are going straight in the wash when I get home. The woman who slept next to me the last hour and a half, the woman who punched me, is standing with her back to the door, her dark hair wild, her brown eyes wilder, and her chest heaving as if she just ran a marathon.

"Right," she says, putting her hands on her hips. "I'm really sorry I punched you."

"Okay."

Air whooshes out of her and her brows scrunch up in confusion. "Okay?"

"Well, I've sort of been working on the assumption that you didn't do it on purpose. I did wake you from what appeared to be a pretty deep sleep." I know from experience how hard it can be to come back to the real world when woken from certain dreams.

I'm still sitting on the toilet, one hand on the sink and the other on the wall, and the woman occupies all available floor space. I have to look up at her, quite far up, and the fact that she's clearly agitated and has already shown aggressive tendencies makes me nervous. I don't really think she'll punch me again but my subconscious isn't convinced.

My words seem to calm her down a little. Her shoulders lower a fraction and her eyes focus on mine instead of skipping all over me like she's watching someone playing pinball on my body.

"Oh," she says. "I *didn't* do it on purpose. I've never hit anyone in my life." Her shoulders go even lower. "I can't believe I had to start today of all days."

Even though she has calmed down, I'm horribly uncomfortable in my current position. Her hands are too close to my still-throbbing face.

Using the sink and the wall for support, I pull myself up. My knees stay bent at a rather uncomfortable angle around the toilet—I don't really have a choice or my chest would be pushing the woman against the door—but I still reach a position where *I'm* looking down on *her* and not the other way around.

She freezes up completely. Her hands go from fluttery to plastered against the door behind her. Her eyes go from apologetic and warm to frozen in what I think is fear. Her breathing stops altogether.

I sit back down.

She takes a shaky breath. But the fear is still there.

I don't like being the one who put it there. Without thinking, I say the first thing that comes to mind. "I've never understood how people do the whole mile-high club thing. There's not even room for two people to stand in here."

Mental face-palm. Next time I want to calm a woman down while we're in a tiny space together, perhaps I won't talk about sex.

It doesn't seem to freak her out, though. Her hands are unglued from the door and her eyebrows climb up her forehead over eyes that are now wide in surprise rather than fear.

She bursts out laughing.

I let out a relieved sigh.

"I'm so sorry," she says. "I'm a mess today and you keep paying for it."

"Don't worry about it. Could have happened to anyone. I appreciate the apology." My hand goes to my cheek to check on the swelling. Yup, getting worse. Going back to work on Monday should be fun.

Her hand lifts as if to touch my cheek, then she changes her mind and her hand falls back down to her side. "God, this is, like, the worst timing ever."

I look up at her. "Why? Is there a *good* time to be punched in the face?"

She snorts a laugh. "Good point. No, I mean it's Valentine's Day tomorrow. If you have a significant other waiting for you at the airport, *I'm* the one who's going to get punched."

My mind offers up the image of Vincent seeing the shiner, getting indignant because it will ruin our romantic date of watching *Le Père Noël est une Ordure* over pizza, and punching this woman in the face. It's so ridiculous, I burst out laughing.

She doesn't laugh with me, so I explain, "There's no significant other waiting for me at the airport. Just a friend who will find this hilarious. He'll probably take pictures and send them to all our friends before we're outside the terminal."

I sigh. "I'm never going to live this down, actually." I catch sight of my glasses in my hand and unfold them, suddenly curious about the damage.

"Shit, your glasses!" She runs a hand through her wild hair. "I totally ruined them. You have to let me pay for repairs. Or new ones. Please?"

I hold the glasses up against the light. "It might not be needed. Nothing seems to be downright broken. Just one branch and one pad bent out of shape. The optician might be able to fix that for free." I shrug. "And if I need new ones, the insurance will pay for it."

She seems disappointed for some reason. Did she want me to be more hurt than I am?

"Please let me help," she says. "To make it up to you in some way. I'll pay for a visit to the doctor. I'll get you makeup to cover up the shiner until it goes away. I'll punch your friend so he won't make fun of you for being hit by a girl."

A huge smile spreads across my face. "Now, *that* is an idea I could get on board with. Except then you'd feel bad again for punching *him* and you'd be back to square one."

She smiles back at me, and I'm suddenly short of breath. "Yeah, I wouldn't actually have gone through with that one," she says. "But I really would like to make it up to you, somehow."

The no smoking sign goes on, indicating we're about to land. We'll have to get out of the lavatory and back to our seats.

I realize I'm sad that in fifteen minutes we'll go our separate ways. And my mouth takes action without checking in with my brain again. "How about you give me your number? That way, I can contact you if I should need anything from you for the glasses or whatever." I flash the grin that my mother claims can get me out of any trouble. "And it should shut my friend up quite nicely."

FOUR

Working on Joining the Mile-High Club

Isabelle

WHAT JUST HAPPENED?

He wants my number? Is it really so he'll be able to contact me if he has any issues with his glasses or is it his idea of a smooth move?

Would anybody want to flirt with a woman who just punched him in the face for no good reason?

I might have been out of the dating game for a while, but that doesn't sound right to me. So it probably is a just-in-case scenario.

I open my mouth to reply but that's as far as I get. The flight attendants decide we've been in here long enough and are pounding on the door to get us to come out. I think I hear one of them saying they have the key and they're not afraid to use it.

They're probably worried we're working on joining the mile-high club. I stifle a laugh at the thought.

Or they're worried I'm in here beating the guy to a pulp, finishing what I started in our seats earlier. Not laughing at that.

I turn around and slide the lock open. I slip out, ignoring the angry stares of the three flight attendants and start walking toward my seat.

"Monsieur, would you like us to find you another seat for the rest of the flight?" I hear one of them saying. Shame spreads through my chest, making my steps heavy.

"I'm good, thanks," the guy replies lightly. "We've got everything sorted out, no worries. Just a misunderstanding."

The weight lifts from my chest and as I wait for him to climb into his window seat, we exchange a smile.

Maybe this day won't be a total disaster, after all.

"I'm Isabelle, by the way," I say as I buckle up my seatbelt. I'm getting tired of thinking of him as "the guy" in my head, and offering my name feels a tad less forward than asking him for his.

"Thomas." It's the first time I see him smile fully, and it makes something tighten in my chest. It's the kind of smile that takes over his entire face, transforming a serious-looking adult into a fun-loving teenager. His teeth are pearly white and perfect—except for one canine that is adorably crooked.

He offers his hand and I shake it. I hope my hands aren't too clammy. That my grip isn't too desperate and strong, or too scared and feeble. His grip is perfect as his large hand envelops mine.

My heart does a little *thump* in my chest.

Oh, my. This really isn't the right time for this.

In fact, *never* would probably be the right time for this. And it has nothing to do with the guy sitting next to me—Thomas, he has a name now—or the fact that I just punched him in the face. It has to do with me needing to figure out what to do with my life. Who I am. What I can do on my own.

Love at First Flight

I've been part of a couple, one where I was most definitely not calling the shots, for so long that I don't even know if I'll be able to function on my own.

And until I figure that out, I can't have some new guy come along and take Pierre's place, telling me what to do, what to think, what to feel. I can't even toy with the idea, or let my overactive imagination get ahold of it, or I'll fall down the rabbit hole I'm trying to climb out of and who knows if I'll have the will or energy to try to get back out another time.

So, beautiful smile and sparking blue eyes notwithstanding, I let go of Thomas's hand and give him a polite smile in return.

I realize it should be my turn to say something now. I'm the one who started this conversation, if it can even be called that. But my mind draws a complete blank. As the plane dips into the layer of clouds and I catch a glimpse of the tops of the Pyrenees bathed in the light of the setting sun in the distance, the fear and excitement of the past fifteen minutes have dissipated, and in their place, I find the usual dread, doubt, and uncertainty.

What am I supposed to do with my life? At thirty-four years old, I'm returning home to my parents with nothing but a large handbag and several kilos of chocolate and sweets. I've run away from my husband of twelve years, I've run away from my job, my friends.

I'm back to square one, except with a lot more baggage.

At some point, I'll have to turn my phone back on and find the inevitable messages from Pierre.

Will I have the strength not to answer?

"So, uh, are you going home to Toulouse, or are you visiting?" Thomas's smile is gone and his voice has a definite hesitance that wasn't there earlier, so he must have noticed my change of mood, but he's not offended or angry, I don't think.

I honestly feel like just ignoring him. I don't have the energy to be polite right now. My world is falling apart and in less than an hour I'll have to face my parents' inevitable speeches of "I told you so." But Thomas's eye is turning blue as we speak. Turning blue because I was skittish even in my sleep, and clocked him when he tried to wake me.

And apart from a short moment of grumpiness at the very first, he's been a complete gentleman about it, not yelling or hitting back or even showing a hint of anger. He has shown compassion and understanding—and is currently trying to make polite conversation.

The least I can do is be polite in return.

"Going home," I reply.

"And is that…" He seems to hesitate. "In Toulouse?"

I nod. "The Busca neighborhood." Normally, I wouldn't tell strangers where I live, but the neighborhood is big enough that he won't be able to find me with only that to go on, and besides, I really don't believe he's asking for the wrong reasons.

"Classy." He flashes his crooked tooth again, and I melt a little.

"It's where my parents live," I explain. "I could never afford to live there." In fact, I can't afford to live *anywhere*, which is why I'm going home with my tail between my legs.

He touches a hand to his darkening cheekbone in a gesture that seems mostly subconscious. I feel a twitch of guilt in my gut and wonder how long the memories from today will haunt me. I feel guilty when I kill spiders. Chances of me easily getting over punching someone are slim to none.

"I'm on Jolimont, myself," he says. "Not as fancy, but it has a killer view."

If he's on the city's only hill and has a view, I can imagine.

He opens his mouth to add something, then shuts it again. I wonder what he was going to say. A quick shake of his head, and he clears his throat. "So, home to visit the parents, then. Planning on staying long?"

My face falls as reality comes crashing back once again. As if on cue, the plane descends into the clouds and we go from having a view of a beautiful blue sky to nothing but gray. That's what the future looks like for me. Gray and obscure and scary.

"Forever," I say, realizing too late that my tone reflects my feeling of doom. It sounds like I'm doing the voice-over to the movie of my own horrible death.

Thomas's face falls. His gaze shifts left and right as if looking for help—or a way out.

Oh shit, he's afraid I'm going to start hitting him again.

It's the last drop. I can't take anymore.

My life is falling apart, my husband is going to be pissed when he realizes to what extent I've left him, my parents are going to judge me for my choices and probably make itemized lists of where I went wrong and why, I have no job and no hope of getting a recommendation from my last one since I just stopped showing up with no warning, a few minutes ago I punched a perfectly innocent guy who had the misfortune of sitting next to me on the plane, and now he thinks I'm a terrible person.

The first tear streaks down my cheek.

And I start spilling my guts.

FIVE

Does it Even Count If He Doesn't Know?

Thomas

THAT LONE TEAR is the only warning I get. I'm not ready, I have no idea how to deal with this, and I'm stuck in my seat until we land.

So I go with the only option available: I listen.

"I'm running back to my parents because I have nowhere else to go." She sobs, followed by a hiccup, then a shaky breath. "I just left my husband of twelve years. Took off with whatever I could think of to grab in five minutes, got on the first plane out of the country, not even caring where as long as it was in Europe, and didn't even leave a note."

She stares sightlessly at the seat in front of her, tears now falling freely from both eyes. I'm not entirely certain she realizes they're there. She certainly makes no move to swipe them away.

"What if he doesn't even know I've left?" Her whisper conveys a level of horror I can't quite link to the words she's saying. "What if he comes home from his work weekend and goes straight to bed? He'll think I'm sleeping in the guest room again. And *tomorrow*." Her eyes widen and her mouth opens and closes a couple of times before she finds her voice again. "He'll just get up really early and assume I'm not up yet, and *go to work*."

She grabs my hand so suddenly, I literally jump in my seat. The blonde flight attendant up front looks at me with a question in her eyes—clearly, she's been keeping an eye on us.

I meet her gaze and give a subtle shake of my head. I'm fine, no need to worry about any more punches.

I hope.

Isabelle's wide eyes are focused on me now. Her grip borders on painful. "What if he *never* realizes I've left? Does it even count, if he doesn't know?"

"I, uh… If your husband doesn't realize you're missing, he's not a very good husband." I have no idea if it's the right thing to say, but she's clearly expecting some sort of answer.

"He's not!" she yells.

The flight attendant's hand is on her harness. She's willing to risk her own safety to come save me from the crazy lady. Although I appreciate the sentiment, I really don't want Isabelle to get into any trouble when she's already having a crappy day, so I raise my free hand in an *I'm fine* gesture and offer a reassuring smile.

My right hand is being slowly crushed into oblivion on the armrest. I try to squeeze back, hoping she'll think I'm acknowledging her and not simply attempting to save an appendage.

Isabelle realizes she's drawing people's attention. After a dirty look toward the flight attendant, she hunches down in her seat in an attempt to hide, and lowers her voice. "My husband was a *terrible* husband. That's why I left him."

I get the feeling she needs confirmation of some sort, so I nod. I don't know her husband, I don't know if he's a good guy or a serial killer, but if his wife is in this state after living with him for twelve years... Yeah, he's probably not a good husband.

"But he has to *know* that I left him!" She's whispering to avoid sharing with the entire plane, but the panic in her voice comes through, crystal clear.

"Why does he have to know?" I ask.

"Because otherwise it doesn't count!"

"It doesn't— How... If you've left, he has to realize it at *some* point, surely?"

Isabelle flexes her jaw as she stares intently into my eyes. I barely dare breathe, let alone blink, as I wonder how far into my soul she can see.

I feel like all my thoughts are out in the open, my feelings pulled out for inspection. Will she judge me for what she sees? Will I pass inspection?

"I guess he'll figure it out Monday night at the latest," she says, suddenly completely calm. "We eat together most nights. He *should* notice if I'm not there."

I can't help it, I raise an eyebrow. "*Should?*"

She giggles. Somehow, we've made it past her panic, and she's looking at the situation from enough of a distance to realize how ridiculous it sounds that a husband would go weeks before realizing his wife has left him. Her grip on my hand loosens, and instead of worrying if I'll have to go to the emergency room when we land, I worry about holding hands with a stranger on the plane.

It's been a while since I held hands with a girl—I've kind of missed it.

Isabelle doesn't seem to realize we're still touching. "God, that sounds weird, doesn't it?" She takes a deep breath and lets it back out slowly. "I think I mostly just need a good night's sleep. It's been a very long day and I hardly slept at all last night."

Covering her eyes with her free hand, she groans. "I spent the first half of the day worrying about Pierre discovering I've left, and now I've moved on to worrying he won't discover it. Great. You must think I'm a complete basket case."

The decision to go with humor isn't quite conscious, or thought through—but then my decisions rarely are. I flash my best smile and nod toward the blonde flight attendant. "She certainly thinks you are. I, on the other hand," I rush to add before she can take offense, "think you're handling this admirably. Leaving someone you've shared your life with for twelve years can't be easy, and from the looks of it, you've been doing it alone?"

I don't voice the thought, but seriously, didn't she have any friends where she lived who could come and help her out? Bring her home to Toulouse? Help her pack more than a carry-on? I'm no expert, but there are times in life when you need friends to lean on, and deciding to leave your spouse definitely qualifies.

Her next breath is shaky but her brown eyes never leave mine. They're steady and present and promise a depth that scares me a little. She might think she's falling apart, but I can tell she's made of sterner stuff. I think I can see the reflection of her entire life's story in those eyes, and it looks like one hell of a ride.

The connection between us is almost too much.

She has captured my attention to the point where I forget we're on a plane. I'm jolted back to the present when the plane touches the ground—twice, maybe because the pilot is as distracted as I am—and reflexively pull my hand free.

I regret it instantly.

But now she has realized we were holding hands for the past ten minutes, I can't go back. That would be awkward. *More* awkward.

We sit there in silence while the plane rushes down the runway and taxis toward the terminal. I hardly spare a glance at the huge Beluga transporter planes on the Airbus side of the runway, even though I usually stay glued to the window to admire those oddly shaped lumps that somehow manage to fly so gracefully while loaded with parts of other planes.

My attention is entirely on Isabelle, even without looking at her. Her heat next to me. The small space that separates our hands on our thighs. The smell of her rosy perfume.

I touch a hand to my cheek and wince when I'm reminded of the shiner—and the cause.

Isabelle's eyes follow the movement of my hand. "I'm *so* sorry I hit you," she says in a whisper.

"I know," I say. "Don't worry about it."

"Still… If there's *anything* I can do to make it up to you…"

I open my mouth to remind her that I already asked for her number and that that would be a great way to make it up to me, when the fasten seatbelts sign is switched off. Seatbelts unfasten, people jump out of their seats, open the overhead compartments, take out their bags…

Even though neither of us gets up immediately, it puts an effective end to our conversation, especially when a "helpful" old man dumps Isabelle's bags in her lap.

Her carry-on is big for a carry-on, but small for something that supposedly contains all of her earthly possessions at the moment. The shopping bag is full of chocolate and sweets.

She sees me noticing. I could have made a joke—normally, I would have made a joke—but I refrain. Chocolate is supposed to be good for heartbreak, isn't it?

Five minutes later, we exit the plane. The old man holds a spot for Isabelle so she can get out of her seat and exit before him, but clearly gallantry doesn't apply to men in their thirties, so I have to wait for most of the plane to empty before anyone lets me out.

By the time I make it into the terminal, Isabelle is long gone.

SIX

Coffee, Aftershave, and Simon

Isabelle

I swear I wasn't planning on running away.

I was going to walk through the terminal with Thomas, tell him goodbye properly, get a last look at his captivating blue eyes, and take off into the sunset.

But then I end up exiting the plane way ahead of him, and standing around waiting for a perfect stranger in the hallways of the terminal just feels too odd. So I move along with the rest of the passengers, through hallway after hallway, past the passport control, more hallways, and all the way to the baggage claim.

Of course, I don't have any baggage to claim. And Thomas knows it. So if I stand here and wait for him, he'll know it was purely to see him again.

The thought sends me almost running through customs and out of the building.

I can't put myself in a situation where I give a guy any kind of power over me. Not when I've finally found the courage to leave Pierre. Thomas seems like a good guy, but I can't risk it.

So I send out a silent apology to the guy who was so nice to me, even after I punched him for no reason, and try to figure out what the next step is.

I have to get to my parents' place. I haven't been home in a few years and when I did come, my parents usually came and picked us up. Now I have to figure out the public transport, which unfortunately has a reputation of being particularly bad around the airport in this city. But I do believe there's supposed to be a new tramway…

"Isabelle!" The shout comes from behind me. I recognize the voice but surely it can't be—

"Simon!" It's all I can get out before I'm enfolded in my brother's arms, my face buried in his large chest, my arms going around his waist by pure reflex.

He smells of coffee, aftershave, and Simon. Like safety.

"What are you doing here?" My voice is muffled by his black winter jacket but there's no way I'm pulling out right away. First I have to get my emotions under control. I came here to be safe, to get away from Pierre, to come home—but I hadn't actually expected to find *home*.

My childhood wasn't miserable by any means. My parents weren't abusive, they paid for any activity I wanted to do, they brought me to all the extra-curricular activities I wanted. But there was still something missing, something that made me feel like I wasn't quite good enough.

My brother never made me feel like that. He's six years my junior, so we didn't play together all that much, or hang out much, really. But he was there. He grew up in the same environment, with the same rules, with the same pressure to always strive for *more*.

It's like we survived the same battlefield.

We never really talked about it much, but it was definitely implied. We might annoy each other, or tease and laugh like most siblings, but it was never more than skin deep. When one of us had what might appear like an overreaction to something our parents did, the other understood. When one of us needed the other, we were there.

And here he is.

"How did you know?" I keep talking into his jacket, pulling him even closer, considering the possibility of never going back out into the real world.

I didn't contact him when I fled my home and pointed my nose toward Toulouse. It's not because I don't trust him, but because I know he's been going through some stuff of his own lately, and I didn't want to burden him with my mess of a life too.

"Mom told me you were coming home," he answers, his voice soft and for my ears only. "Asked me to get your room ready. She said you were planning on taking public transport to get home but I figured that was just to avoid asking a favor of Mom."

I sniffle, attempting to pass it off as a laugh. Simon isn't fooled, but he'll probably let me pretend.

"That bag all you got?" he says.

I sigh. "Yeah. I have about three changes of clothes, my computer and some other tech stuff, my e-reader, and about a ton of chocolate."

His rumbling chuckle vibrates right through my body. "Sounds like you have everything you need. We'll plan for some shopping tomorrow—and an overdose of chocolate tonight. Rerun of *Friends*? Or *Game of Thrones*?"

Love at First Flight

I free one arm to wipe at my face, making sure I get rid of the last stray tears. I think some of them might be from the flight, when I suddenly spewed all my weird fears to Thomas, ensuring he'd forever think of me as "that weird woman from the plane who punched me."

"Definitely *Friends*," I say, even managing a laugh. "No thinking, no violence, please."

"You got it." Pulling back, Simon studies my face and I know he notices the puffy eyes, the dark rings under my eyes, the signs of recent crying. "I'm taking at least half of the chocolate, though, as payment for coming to get you."

As I burst out laughing, some of the weight that has accumulated on my shoulders for so long lifts a little. I feel like maybe I can do this. Simon is here with me, so we'll find a solution. "Hey!" I pretend-slap him on the chest. "That's heartbreak chocolate, paid for with my hard-earned money in Amsterdam. What makes you think I'll share?"

Grabbing my carry-on in one hand, Simon slings the other arm over my shoulder and pulls me toward the parking lot. "You don't have monopoly on heartbreak, you know," he says lightly.

"Oh no, what happened? Is this why you're in Toulouse? You were already here?"

"That's a story for another day," he replies lightly. He smiles, and it's a good one, but I know him well enough to see the pain behind it. "Right now, we're focusing on you."

We wait in line behind a family of four so Simon can pay for the parking at one of the machines by the main entrance and I can't stop staring at his face. His hair is as dark as mine but with more curls, something that is more obvious than usual since he's let his grow out a little. His eyes are the same dark brown as mine but the shape is closer to almond like Dad, where I tend toward round like Mom. He's grown a scruff, like so many guys these days, and it suits him. Makes him look…adult. I smile at my own thought. It's weird thinking about my little brother as an adult, even when he's almost thirty.

Simon steps up to the machine and pays for the hour he's apparently been here. "So, how was your flight?" he asks.

It's supposed to be a simple question, what you ask of anyone who's traveled.

But today, it's not, of course. "I punched a guy in the face," I say. I still feel absolutely awful about it, but I'm also amused at being able to surprise my brother like this.

He doesn't disappoint. He does a quick check and sees the amusement—and not fear—on my face, then barks out a laugh so loud several people waiting in line to pay turn to see what's going on. "You did *what*? How did you manage that?"

I grab his hand and we walk toward the car. "Get me home, and I'll tell you all about it."

SEVEN

You Find This Charming?

Thomas

"What the hell happened to you?" Vincent's jaw is slack as he takes in my increasingly impressive shiner. I never did put anything other than the tepid tissues on it, so I'm guessing it's going to be with me for a while.

In the midst of the crowd outside customs, I shake Vincent's hand. He's wearing his usual ridiculous red winter beanie, complete with ginormous pom-pom that sways from side to side when he moves. His grandmother made it for him for Christmas four years ago and the first time he wore it, a silly girl who couldn't be more than nineteen told him he looked ridiculous. Out of pure spite—or, as the official story goes, because he would never want to attract that type of girl anyway—he's worn that beanie all through winter ever since. I've learned to ignore the stares.

I am, however, increasingly aware of people's eyes on *me* right now. My friend's exclamation isn't helping matters. A couple with two young kids move a few steps away from me, the mother giving me a proper stink-eye. A man who can't be more than thirty but clearly considers himself very important seeing the suit and tie he's wearing, looks down his nose at me, as if I started a bar fight and he can't believe someone would do something so plebeian.

One elderly lady who was a few rows ahead of me on my flight whispers into the ear of her equally old husband—I *hope*, explaining that I did *not* start a fight, that I will *not* be saying anything in the vein of "you should see the other guy."

I look around the arrival hall quickly, hoping against hope to see a woman with dark hair and soulful brown eyes.

No such luck, of course. Isabelle must have been through here thirty minutes ago, seeing how she didn't have any bags to retrieve.

Unsurprisingly, I didn't have a bag to retrieve either. But I had to wait for a small eternity by the conveyor belts, watching everybody else grab their things, until the "last bag on belt" sign came up—at which point I got to stand in line for ten more minutes to describe how my bag looks, what's in it, do I have anything to declare in customs... Only to learn that yes, they knew where my suitcase was. In Toulon. Apparently, the clerk who took my bag on departure couldn't tell the difference between Toulouse and Toulon.

They claim I'll get my suitcase by the end of the next day.

I start walking and pull on Vincent's hand before letting it go, so we can move away from the crowd. "I got punched in the face on the plane," I explain, keeping my tone light.

Yes, I'm going to take this opportunity to mess with my friend. Duh.

"On the plane?" Vincent seems equally horrified and thrilled. The pom-pom on his beanie bounces wildly as he whips around to stare at me. "By who? Why?"

"By the person sitting next to me. Didn't appreciate being woken up."

Vincent laughs out loud. "You woke up some dude while he was sleeping? I'd have punched you too, man." He slaps my shoulder.

I feign righteous defensiveness. "It was just before we landed. That nap was about to end anyway. And it wasn't a guy."

I keep walking, passing the sliding doors leading out of the terminal and straight into the four-level parking lot where Vincent always parks. I pretend not to notice when he stops in his tracks.

"Not a guy? You got punched by a *girl*?"

I turn, walk back to pull him along toward his car. "I don't think she qualifies as a girl. Woman would be more exact." I nod, as if agreeing with my own assessment.

"Who gets punched by a *woman* on a flight? What the hell did you do to wake her up?" Vincent is enjoying himself now. I can practically see him composing his own version of the story, to be told and retold whenever we get together with our old college friends.

"Nothing!" I raise both hands, palms out. "I promise. I was a perfect gentleman who just so happened needed to get out of his seat, and therefore wake his neighbor up to get past. She, uh, didn't understand my intent straight away."

We've reached Vincent's old and battered Peugeot 106. He's had this car since we were students—and that isn't as recent as we'd like to think. I suspect him of having a special deal with a mechanic somewhere for this wreck to pass inspections every year. The passenger door is red instead of blue like the rest of the car, from when it popped open all by itself while he was driving on the highway about five years back. The passenger door hit a truck and was well beyond repair when Vincent found it hours later. The car's a death trap but we keep using it anyway.

Vincent pauses by the driver's side, with one hand on the roof of the car. "She really just punched you?"

I shrug. "It's not a big deal, all right? She was having a bad day and didn't know where she was when she woke up."

"Where did she think she was?"

From what she told me, I can imagine, and I don't like what I see. Even though I'll probably never meet Isabelle again, and there's about zero chance of Vincent knowing who she is if *he* runs into her, I keep my thoughts to myself, so I simply offer a shrug. I'm not sure if her tearful outpouring of woe on the plane constitutes a confession, and most of the passengers around us also heard it, but it was definitely private. I'm not sharing it with anyone.

I throw my carry-on into the back seat and get into the passenger seat. Vincent gets in behind the wheel but doesn't start the car straight away. He just sits there with his hands in his lap, the pom-pom of his beanie brushing the car's roof, and his mouth hanging open, staring at me.

"You *liked* this woman," he says. He seems surprised, but also gleeful—I'm going to hear about this for *such* a long time. "A woman punches you in the face, giving you a gigantic shiner, probably breaking your glasses since you're not wearing them—and you find this *charming*?"

I cross my arms. "I did not use the word charming. Nor did I say I like her."

"But you do." Vincent puts the key in the ignition. "You liked her. Did you get her number?" His face is right in front of mine, watching for a reaction, while he throws an arm behind my seat to watch where he's going as he backs out of the space. The car shudders, like it always does when the reverse is first engaged.

Then we're out and aiming for the exit.

We drive in silence until we're halfway to my apartment. "She wouldn't give me her number," I mumble. "And when we deplaned, she just disappeared."

Vincent throws me a glance, a compassionate smile playing on his lips. "Don't worry about it, man. You'll meet someone else soon. Someone who won't punch you."

"Where's the fun in that?"

"Ha! We'll talk again tomorrow, when you've gotten a proper look at your face and it's had some time to settle. And how about we go out for a drink on Friday? Check out the prospects?"

He makes it sound like we're in the habit of going to bars to pick up girls. It couldn't be further from the truth. But it sounds like a decent idea, and after a weekend of fighting with investors, and a whole week of work, it would probably be exactly what the doctor ordered. Minus the checking out of prospects.

"Sounds like a plan," I say.

We pull up in front of my building, the old lady on the ground floor who's always watching the goings-on from her window scowling at us like we're a couple of hooligans planning to set the trash cans on fire. That happened *once* five years ago, some teenagers from the local high school who thought arson would be a fun pastime during their free period, and Madame Gérard has had it in for anyone below the age of forty ever since.

"That shiner's still going to be there on Friday," Vincent muses as he studies my face. He slips one finger under his beanie to scratch the back of his head. "You might want to look into getting some makeup."

I make a half-hearted attempt at giving him a black eye to match mine, but somehow, I miss.

EIGHT

You That Happy to See the Pink Kitten Again?

Isabelle

SEEING MY PARENTS again is much like I anticipated. My mom gives me a hug, my dad a pat on the back. They tell me I can stay with them for as long as I like, my room will always be my room, and that I'm better off without Pierre.

Of course, they've always thought I'd be better off without Pierre. I think it might be a big part of the reason why I stayed with him for so long. If there was one thing I learned growing up, it was never to admit defeat, never to be anything less than perfect. Officially admitting I'd married a jerk…was pretty low on my list of things I wanted to do.

But enough is enough and I've *finally* come to the conclusion that facing my judgmental parents will be better than staying with Pierre.

Which means I should have left him years ago, since this situation was apparently inevitable.

I try my best to steer my thoughts away from downward spirals like that one, but it's not always easy. Especially when my mom looks at me with pity.

"Would you like to talk about it?" she asks me. Her big eyes have always made her look perpetually curious and trustworthy. It's something she takes great advantage of in her job as a lawyer.

Luckily, looking into the same eyes in the mirror every morning, I'm immune. And I'm not about to give her any more ammo. "I really wouldn't," I reply, my tone way beyond grumpy. Took me all of two minutes to be back in I-hate-my-parents mode, making me sound and feel like an ungrateful teenager. So I school my tone as best I can. "I've had a really long day. I'm going to go to bed, if that's all right with you."

I start up the stairs, then stop. "If Pierre should call, can you tell him I'm all right and nothing else, please?"

"Of course, *chérie*," my mom says, her voice thick with hurt and pity.

I flee up to my room.

Where Simon is waiting for me.

"So, I'm guessing, from the look on your face, that went as well as expected?" He's lounging on my twin bed, looking ridiculous on pink kitten-covered sheets.

Another surge of anger rises in me. Sure, those sheets were mine back in the day—but it was *way* back, when I was twelve.

I take a deep breath. Count to five. Let the air back out in a big whoosh.

"You that happy to see the pink kitten again?" Simon teases.

From anybody else, and especially from my parents, that

comment would have made me blow a gasket. From Simon, it makes me smile.

"She thought it might comfort you," Simon says softly. "I know it's a miss, but the thought behind the act really was a good one. She just isn't able to see how it could be taken in any other way than the one she meant it."

I slump into the old beanbag by the window, throwing up a cloud of dust. "She never does try to see things my way."

"I know." A comfortable silence settles and my gaze lazily takes in my old room. They've left everything exactly like I left it when I moved out at eighteen, which means there are posters of boy bands on the walls, pictures of me with my high school friends with hearts drawn on them on the mirror and the corkboard over my desk, and a bookcase full of paperback books, mostly fantasy but with quite a bit of mystery in the mix.

I don't think a single thing has been moved since I left. I wonder if my journal is still in my "secret compartment" under the desk—I'll have to check when Simon leaves.

"So… What made you finally leave Pierre?" Simon is propped up against my headboard, one hand tracing the lines of Hello Kitty on the covers. He's not looking directly at me, but I have no doubt he's employing his every skill to watch me in his peripheral vision.

I lean back in the beanbag until my head hits the radiator. Outside, all I can see is the murky gray sky and the dark windows of the next-door neighbor.

"He genuinely scared me," I whisper.

"How so?" Simon's voice is soft but I know he's ready to take off for England to fight Pierre if I give the word.

I shake my head, my eyes on the swaying palm tree in the neighbor's back yard. "He's been hurting me with his words for years. Nothing too direct, you know? Not, like, 'you're stupid' or 'you're worthless.' But that's still how I felt." A deep sigh. "On some level I've known for a while that I needed to leave, but then there were good days, and I figured leaving everything behind would be stupid, so I stayed."

I shoot a quick glance at Simon, but immediately return to the palm tree. It's safer. "On Saturday, before leaving for a team-building weekend with his colleagues, he threatened me." I pause. "It was still just words, he hasn't laid a hand on me. But he threatened to."

"Why?" Bless Simon for not being outwardly angry on my behalf. It's the reaction any normal person would have, but it doesn't really help. Especially when the offending party is on the other side of the English Channel. *I* need him to be calm, and present.

I stay silent for several moments as I think back to our fight. I can hardly believe it was only yesterday morning. It feels like it was weeks ago, at least. A different life.

"I planned to take another painting course. Silk painting. A friend had told me about it earlier in the week and they had a few open spots, so I figured I'd give it a try. But Pierre didn't want me to go. Thought it was a waste of money. That I'd already spent enough on painting over the past years and why the hell would I paint on silk?"

Simon clicks his tongue. "Seriously, it's like he never knew you at all."

My laugh is mirthless. "Maybe he didn't. He usually tolerates when I do things like this, but for some reason, this was the last straw, I think. He's been pretty busy at work lately. I don't think his company is doing all that well, and he's probably worried about losing his job." This time I meet Simon's gaze head-on. "I know that's not an excuse, all right? That's why I'm here, after all. But it might, kind of, explain why he went further than usual when wanting to put me down."

"So, what, he was going to hit you if you signed up for the painting class?"

I blow a raspberry at how surreal that sounds. "It was like it was taken out of a movie from the fifties or something, or whenever it was acceptable for a man to threaten his wife to get her back in line."

"Well." Simon smacks one of my pillows. It's the best replacement for Pierre he's going to get, so I don't try to stop it. "Good riddance. So I guess you have a bunch of administrative stuff to take care of now?"

I groan. The mere idea of getting out of the beanbag to go to bed feels like too much work—starting the separation process is basically impossible.

"We'll deal with it tomorrow. I'll help out." Simon straightens, only to lie down on my bed with his head right next to mine. "Now, tell me more about this Thomas guy from the plane. I don't understand why you didn't give him your number."

The change of subject is welcome, as is the memory of Thomas as he accepted my apology and held my hand while listening to my nonsensical rant.

But I can't let it distract me too much. As agreeable as it is to daydream about a pretty boy, very much like I used to do in my teenage years right in this spot, I need to stay in real life. I need to properly extract myself from Pierre—not only physically, but administratively too. I'll need to start the separation process, however the hell that works. I'll need my own bank account, transfer money from my old one. Contact my employer to explain why I've disappeared into thin air…

The next few days are not going to be fun.

Simon must read the answer on my face. He reaches out to take my hand in his much larger one. "I'll help you get rid of the current guy first, Isa. *Then* we'll see about finding a suitable replacement."

Thanking the stars I'm blessed with such a wonderful brother, I kiss the back of his hand. We stay that way until we both fall asleep.

NINE

Let the Last One Fade First, at Least

Thomas

My colleagues have several bets going on the state of my black eye. One tries to predict the colors from day to day. The other projects when it will be completely gone.

Clément, the colleague seated the closest to my desk, has put down for three weeks on that last one—he better not be right.

Five days after being punched, I have a dark, almost black, line running along the eye socket under my eye, the line being extra wide right next to my nose. The area between the line and the eye is now green, tending toward yellow. I'm guessing that in a day or two, it'll all be a sickly yellow. The tiny cut on my brow has scabbed over and is already healed, although it's still a little sore when I touch it. My nose still has a hint of the imprint of the pad of my glasses, but nobody else can see that since I'm finally wearing my glasses again.

I'd been right about the optician being able to fix my glasses. Without a second look at my shiner, the kind lady took my glasses to the rear of the shop, bent them back into shape, and returned them to me, good as new, less than two minutes later. I somehow got the feeling that having your glasses shoved into your face wasn't all that uncommon.

The dangers of being nearsighted.

Right now, it's Friday night, and I'm going out with Vincent for a drink. We're not planning on staying out late, or getting drunk, or picking up girls. Just an hour or two to unwind.

And I'm standing in front of my bathroom mirror, considering the merits of Isabelle's offer to help me with makeup. Not that I *can* take her up on it since I never got her number, but I really never thought the idea could appeal to me.

However, I've spent a week with my colleagues looking at me oddly, their gaze never quite meeting mine, but focusing on the ever-evolving color of the skin *under* my eye, all of them clearly wondering what the hell I'd been up to.

No, I did *not* choose to tell my colleagues how I got it.

Maybe it would have made less of a fuss if I had. Or it would have completely undermined my authority since the person who hit me was a woman. I work in a very masculine field, where the male to female ratio is about 80/20, so the idea of explaining to idiots that yes, women can also throw a punch, simply isn't something I want to venture into.

Besides, I never share information about my personal life with my colleagues. I prefer to keep my personal and professional lives separate.

Who knows, maybe the mystery of it all will help my reputation. I'm pretty sure they're imagining me starting a fight with someone. Which is ridiculous. But unfortunately helps with gaining street cred in groups like this one.

And now I'm going to a bar. Even though it's a calm one, it's going to be filled with people I don't know, and they're bound to stare at the shiner, wonder what I've been up to.

Ah well, nothing I can do about it now. Vincent will be here in five minutes and since I don't own any makeup, well, it's going to be difficult using it.

I'll just have to own it.

We've decided on La Lanterne Bleue, a place that looks more like a hipster coffee shop than a bar. The indoor part of the place wouldn't take up more than half of my apartment with less than a handful of tables, but what makes the place special is the back yard. No more than ten meters wide and maybe thirty meters long, the yard is surrounded on all four sides by the red brick walls of surrounding buildings. White-painted windows with pastel-colored shutters and colorful flower boxes look down on us from all three floors, and a large oak tree grows in the very middle. Its roots are pulling away the gray tiles one by one, year after year, but nobody seem to care. Guests are told to watch their step as they cross the yard, and that's that. Not that anyone does, because their eyes are always on the dozens of blue lanterns hung on the branches of the large tree.

Now, it *is* February, and although Toulouse is far from being the coldest city in France, it's also far from *warm*. The bar has set out heating elements at most of the tables, and old-timers like us know to dress accordingly. Which, for Vincent, means red pom-pom beanie, of course.

Bundled up in my winter coat, a blue scarf, and a matching knitted cap—no pom-pom for me, thank you very much—I sip my beer while admiring the gently swinging lights above us. We're at the very back of the yard, which I'm happy with, because nobody ever comes through here. Except the poor souls who have too much beer and need to use the restrooms—not exactly a selling point for the bar. I went once, the very first time we came here, and swore to never open that rickety door again.

Speaking of, a rather solid-looking guy who I'd be willing to bet has been a rugby player at some point in his life, is carefully picking out a route through the tables in our direction. He must be new. I'll make a point of checking out his expression when he comes back out.

"I'm just glad the poor thing didn't have rabies," Vincent says. He's been giving me a run-down of his week, and it appears the culminating event was when someone brought in a stray pup to his veterinary clinic and he somehow managed to get bitten. He claims he jumped in to save the little girl who brought the puppy. I'll give him the benefit of the doubt on this one.

The rugby dude stumbles over one of the roots and comes flying toward our table.

He catches himself just in time, one hand on our table, making our beers wobble. "God, so sorry."

"Don't worry about it," I tell him.

"Maybe go a little lighter on the beer," Vincent tells him, large smile showing he's only teasing, pom-pom bobbing with the movement of his head making it quite clear he's not looking for a fight. "Thomas here doesn't need any new bruises on his pretty face. Let the last one fade first, at least."

Surprise registering on his face, the guy zeroes in on my shiner.

Great. Thank you, Vincent. Nobody has stared for over an hour, so he's pointing it out to strangers.

The guy apologizes again, gives me a once-over, and enters the restroom.

That was odd. Maybe he's gay?

Vincent drones on with his puppy-no-rabies story while I sip on my beer. Less than two minutes later, the guy pops back out of the restroom, a slightly panicked expression on his face—yeah, that place does that to everyone—and he zeroes in on me again as he walks away.

Weird.

Vincent is still on his puppy story five minutes later, and I'm about to get up to get us a second round when another person comes into view, aiming for the restroom. A woman this time. I'd bet anything she'll open the door, have a quick look, and change her mind. I have yet to see any females do anything else.

I empty the last drops of my beer into my mouth as the woman turns her head so her face comes into view.

It's Isabelle.

TEN

Wonderfully Dull and Normal

Isabelle

I'M NOT QUITE sure why I agreed to come out with Simon tonight. Getting away from all the paperwork of separating from Pierre was part of it. Escaping the parents another. Wanting to prove to myself that I can have a life on my own, and do normal and nice things like hanging out with my brother on a Friday night.

But the biggest reason is actually Simon himself. He still hasn't wanted to explain why he's also living at home right now, seemingly as lost and adrift as myself. That's fine with me. He'll tell me when he's ready. But I don't need him to say the words to know that he needs a break from everything as much as I do.

So here we are, in one of the calmest bars of the city, no more than five hundred meters from our parents' house, drinking beer (Simon) and milkshake (me), people-watching, and talking about books we've read recently and movies we want to see.

It all feels wonderfully dull and normal.

After his first beer, Simon excuses himself to go to the bathroom. I open my phone to read some news, not liking sitting there alone with nothing to do. When a waiter comes by, I order another beer for Simon.

Three minutes later, Simon is back. He slips into his seat, out of breath, eyes wide and sparkling with excitement.

"How far did you have to go to find the bathroom?" I ask with a smile.

Simon's responding smile stretches across his face in a way I haven't seen in years, and certainly not in the past week. It's the smile he always wore before doing something he thought was going to be *so* cool but the parents inevitably qualified as stupid.

I'm so glad to see they didn't force that smile out of him completely.

"That restroom was…special," Simon says. "You should go check it out."

I narrow my eyes at him. He never set me up for pranks before, and I don't see him starting now, but this is highly suspicious. "But I don't need to go."

"No need to actually use it." He waves a dismissive hand. "Just pretend, go have a look. Come back."

Yeah, something's definitely up.

I guess it could be a designer restroom or something, and he wants me to see it. That actually happened once when we traveled together to Dresden about ten years back.

So deciding to trust my brother, I get up, throw a last suspicious look at him, and walk toward the back yard.

"It's in the back corner!" Simon yells after me. "You can't miss it!"

The oak tree with its decorations is beautiful. It makes me long for my garden back in England, where I had a tree not that different from this one. I loved sitting in its shade and losing myself in a book in summer. Lanterns like these would have been *perfect*.

I almost trip over a root, so I turn to face where I'm going instead of looking up into the tree.

A brusque movement catches my eye at the table closest to the restroom. A man with glasses stares at me like he's seen a ghost. He has dark hair sticking out from below a blue beanie, a few days' worth of beard, and a big black winter jacket.

I keep walking toward the restroom but I'm slowing down. The guy won't stop staring. Now that I'm closer, I can see his bright blue eyes behind the glasses, and the remnants of a black eye—

"Thomas." I stop in my tracks, right next to three young women who look up at me with quizzical stares. I hardly notice.

The guy I punched is sitting right there. I didn't recognize him straight away because of the glasses but it's definitely him. He's holding an empty glass of beer in one hand. His friend, a guy in a ridiculous red beanie with the world's largest pom-pom, was talking but trails off as his gaze jumps from his friend, to me, and back again.

Several seconds. We're both frozen in place.

The three women start to grumble. I think Thomas's friend says something, but I'm too far away to hear—or it might be because of the buzzing in my ears.

He recovers first. "Isabelle? What are you doing here?"

I let out something that's half-snort, half-hiccup. "Having a drink. What are *you* doing here?" I keep wondering if he's followed me here—except he must have arrived before me because I haven't seen him pass our table.

His smile is stunning. "Having a drink." He holds up his empty glass.

"Thomas," his friend says, pom-pom bobbing. "Would you mind introducing me to your friend?"

Thomas waves me over and somehow, I remember how to make my legs work. I approach their table, but not too close. Awkward doesn't even begin to describe how I'm feeling right now. It's tempting to just keep going and go hide in the restroom.

"Vincent," Thomas says and holds out a hand in my direction. "This is Isabelle, the woman who punched me in the face on my flight from Amsterdam last Sunday." He extends his hand toward Vincent. "Isabelle, this is my friend Vincent. The friend who picked me up at the airport."

"Nice to meet you," I blurt out.

I can feel the blush rising up my throat. My embarrassment is so strong, I'm sure they can see it, even in this dim lighting.

Thomas's smile becomes impossibly wider. He's showing off that crooked tooth again. My heart pinches in my chest. "How polite," he says. "But apparently whoever taught you your manners forgot to mention it's rude to take off without so much as a goodbye."

"Oh God." I cover my face with my hands. I've never been so embarrassed in my life. I would give anything to be anywhere but here.

Almost anywhere. Not England.

A large hand lands on my shoulder and I jump a foot in the air. I even let out a little squeak, before I notice it's only Simon.

"What's keeping you, Isa?" His expression is suspiciously innocent. "Figured I'd come check if you'd fallen in or something."

I simply stare at him. What is he talking about? I can't have been gone for more than a minute. And why does he have our drinks in his other hand?

Thomas's friend—Vincent—clears his throat. He seems to be enjoying himself. "Well, well, well. The plot thickens. And who might you be? The bodyguard she usually sends to do her punching?"

Simon roars with laughter. I'm about to ask him what the hell he's up to when my gaze falls on Thomas. The smile is completely gone and a worry line appears on his forehead. The look he's sending Simon seems to contain both anger and hurt.

I have *no* idea what's going on.

"I'm the brother," Simon says jovially. "So I guess in a way, you're right. If she asks me to go punch someone, I'll probably do it." He studies me through narrowed eyes for a second. "Though I might need to ask for a justification first. She *apparently* throws around punches for no good reason when I'm not there to watch her."

Vincent says something back, but I zone him out completely. The minute Simon said he is my brother, Thomas perked up. Like, literally straightened his spine, worry line gone, leaning forward in his chair.

Really? Am I reading this correctly? Saying my flirting is rusty would be something of an understatement, but I'd be willing to bet Thomas's behavior means he's interested. In me.

How is that even possible? I *punched* him, for crying out loud. For no good reason, as my brother so kindly pointed out.

Simon nudges my shoulder. "What do you say, Isa?"

I tear my eyes away from Thomas and look uncomprehendingly at my brother.

"Should we join them?" He points to Vincent, who is already pulling over two chairs from a nearby table. The metal scrapes against the tiles, not helping with clearing up the jumble in my head in the slightest.

My gaze falls to our glasses in Simon's hand. How did he know? What's he doing?

"Come on," he says gently. He sets our glasses on the table and pulls me toward the chairs with one arm slung protectively over my shoulder. "This way you can apologize one more time. Make sure he's okay. Be dazzled by his pretty smile." That last was, luckily, whispered directly into my ear.

I *knew* I shouldn't have told him about the smile. Never give brothers ammo.

I sink into the chair, the cold from the metal seeping through my jeans in seconds. My eyes stay on my folded hands as I search for words.

I can't find any.

ELEVEN

It Can't Get Any Weirder Than This

Thomas

THE BROTHER IS the guy who used the restroom just minutes ago. Somehow, he must have known who I am and that's why he kept staring at me. Then he apparently sent Isabelle back here so we could bump into each other. Surely, I can't be the only guy in all of Toulouse with a black eye?

I brush that thought aside. It's not important. What is important is that I'm going to assume this means she *wants* to talk to me again, that she has somehow said something positive to him about our encounter.

I guess this *could* be a prank on the brother's part. Siblings are known to put each other through the wringer, after all. But even though Isabelle seems embarrassed and awkward as hell, I think she trusts him. She leans toward him slightly, as if seeking out his strength.

She's as beautiful as I remember. Even more so without dark circles under her eyes, her hair in order, and some of that panic gone. Which doesn't mean she's at ease. Her dark hair hangs forward like a curtain, almost hiding her from view, as she wrings her hands in her lap.

And now I regret teasing her. I blame Vincent. He always brings out the stupid in me.

"I'm sorry to have teased you just now," I tell her gently. "I understand that you wanted to get home as soon as possible after the day you'd had. No hard feelings, I promise."

Her head lifts and her soulful dark eyes meet mine. Anguish mixed with appreciation. "I'm sorry I didn't say goodbye. When I got off the plane, you weren't there, and then… And… I'm so sorry I punched you!"

The brother puts a large hand on her shoulder, giving it a squeeze. I think he might be fighting a smile.

"You already apologized on the plane," I remind her. "Several times. And I accepted the apology, remember?"

Only when her eyes widen and her gaze lowers to her hands do I realize I've put my hand on hers in an attempt to comfort her. I snatch my hand away.

Then regret it when dismay spreads across her features. I'm clearly the epitome of smooth today. Just like every day. Sigh.

The brother places his half-empty beer glass on the table and puts Isabelle's milkshake into her hands. "Now that the apologies are out of the way… Tell me, Thomas, what do you do for a living?"

I watch as Isabelle's lips close around the straw of her milkshake and can't remember what I do for a living.

"Something to do with computers," I croak out.

"That's…" The brother clears his throat and I think I hear Vincent snickering but I can't tear my eyes away from Isabelle to check. "Something to do with computers. That doesn't bode very well for your clients. Or are you dumbing it down for us?"

The hint of anger in his tone finally snaps me out of the spell Isabelle and her straw have me under. Great plan, Thomas. Insult the girl's jock brother.

"I'm not dumbing it down, I promise." I sigh. "I'm the one who turns dumb when it's Friday night and my work week is finally over. I'm a senior manager in a small IT company. We specialize in mobile apps, particularly anything to do with food or arts."

Simon studies me intently for several moments, but he seems to accept my explanation. Sensitive about being judged because of his size: noted.

"What kind of food and arts apps are we talking about?" My heart jumps into my throat when Isabelle speaks. She's not meeting my eyes, instead focusing on the twirling of her straw in her milkshake, but that suits me just fine. I think staring into those eyes for too long will fry my brain as quickly as her lips on that straw did.

I don't usually like talking about work on the weekend, but I find that when Isabelle is the one asking the questions, I'm fine with it. I do not miss Vincent's snort when I start talking.

"We have one app for sharing recipes, searching the web for similar ones, finding one with what you have in your fridge, that sort of stuff. Then there's one listing all the restaurants in your area, with menus and reviews and the possibility to make reservations.

"In the arts, we don't have all that much at the moment, but we're working on it. We're trying to branch out. We're about to release one that's similar to the restaurant one, where you can find the closest museum or art gallery, know what artists you can find there, reserve tickets… We're trying to get a foothold in the field, but where all our employees adore eating and had a ton of ideas of features to implement on the food apps, I'm afraid we're a lot poorer in this area. Let's say it's a work in progress."

I'm doing my best to ignore the shit-eating grin on Vincent's face across the table, which would have been a lot easier if that giant red pom-pom didn't draw the eye every time he moves his head. Yeah, yeah, when he asks me questions about my work, getting answers is like pulling teeth. I don't even care. He already knows I like this woman. I'm just going to hope he'll wait until we're alone to start on the teasing.

Isabelle has listened to my every word, but her brother is the one who pulls out his phone. "So I can download your apps right now if I want? What are they called?"

He opens the app store and tips the phone in my direction. Knowing better than to take someone's phone out of their hand, I lean forward to type in the name of our most popular food app. The one that can produce a recipe from a list of ingredients is very popular with the young crowd.

I catch a whiff of rose and am suddenly brought back to the plane lavatory. The smell of Isabelle's hair as we were locked into that tiny space together. How hard she insisted on apologizing. How vulnerable she suddenly was when I tried to get up and towered over her.

"Your app's name is weird." The brother's voice cuts into my daydream and my focus snaps back to the phone in his hand. Where I've typed the first four letters of our app's name—followed by fifteen to twenty repetitions of the letter f.

Starting to wonder if there's any hope for me at all, I lean back, out of reach of Isabelle's tantalizing aroma, and manage a weak laugh. "Sorry, got distracted. Just, uh, remove all those extra letters and replace them with a u."

Simon flashes a grin that tells me he knows *exactly* what's going on. While he taps on his phone, he elbows his sister. "I like this one, Isa. I think he passes muster." I see the welcome screen of our app on his phone. "Oh, food! I'm hungry."

Isabelle is cringing so badly I'm afraid she might fall off her chair. The straw in her milkshake is chewed out of shape to the point where there are pieces missing. I hope she didn't swallow them.

Before I can say anything to reassure her, my own wingman decides to jump into the fray. "I could eat!" A look passes between Vincent and the brother and suddenly they both jump into action.

"There's a pizza place down the street." The brother brandishes his phone. "Says so right here in the app! How do you feel about duck breast on your pizza?" He's tapping away, already ordering, from the looks of it.

"I don't want to eat, Simon," Isabelle pleads with her brother. "I told you I just wanted a milkshake." Her voice is quivering. It makes me want to wrap her up in my arms and tell her everything is going to be all right.

Except I'm pretty sure I'm the reason she's freaking out, so nothing I do is going to help right now.

The brother, who should know his sister well enough to read the signs of distress, ignores Isabelle completely. "That's all right, Isa. Why don't you stay here with Thomas? He doesn't seem hungry, either. Me and my new friend Vincent, here, are going to grab a couple of pizzas, then we'll be back to pick you up in, say, an hour?"

He's not looking at his sister as he asks this, but at my best friend.

Who nods in reply, shit-eating grin in place. "Yeah, that sounds about right. You'll watch over the man's sister, won't you, Thomas?"

This earns him three scowls. Yeah, Vincent isn't so good with being eloquent, either.

I can't think of anything to say that will end well for me. If I agree to watch Simon's sister for him, I'm no better than Vincent. If I say I'm also hungry, I'm basically leaving Isabelle in the lurch. If I suggest for all of us to go together, I'm forcing Isabelle to go along.

If I tell them I'd like nothing more than to have an hour alone with Isabelle, I'd be too honest.

My self-preservation rules that one out.

In the end, I say nothing, and my non-action becomes an action. Simon and Vincent quickly gulp down the rest of their drinks, grab their things, and wave quick goodbyes as they practically run out of the bar.

Isabelle lets out a sound that might be a whimper. "It can't get any weirder than this."

I, of course, reply without thinking. "It's right up there with getting punched by a stranger out of the blue."

TWELVE

Overly Helpful Wingmen

Isabelle

OH, THE HORROR.

How is this my life? Is it not enough admitting that your twelve-year-long relationship was rotten? To start from scratch at thirty-four? Living in my childhood room with boy bands on my walls? No, I also have to add in assaulting a perfectly innocent and nice man for no good reason, and then piling up the embarrassing moments whenever he's near. Which is more often than you'd think.

Seriously, Simon just *left* me here? And with such subtlety.

When Thomas makes his jab about me hitting him, I reach my limit. I put my almost-empty glass on the table and start getting up—

"I'm so sorry." Thomas leans forward, into my personal space. His hand is on mine again, and this time when I look down at our joined hands, he doesn't pull away. "I'm very good at coming up with biting or idiotic comments, which is a real asset when goofing around with my stupid friends, but not so much when interacting with people in the real world."

When it's clear I'm not actually getting up, he adds his other hand, enfolding my hand in a nice, warm cocoon. "I meant what I said. I don't blame you for hitting me, at all. Please, let that go, okay?" He looks like he's about to add something, then thinks better of it.

I feel ridiculous in my almost-rising-from-my-seat position, so I ease back to actually resting my ass on the chair. It's sort of warm now. I guess it has siphoned off all the heat I'm radiating because of embarrassment.

"Your brother seems nice," Thomas says.

Now that it's just the two of us, and things are calming down a little, I take in Thomas's eyes for the first time today. They're as sparkling blue as I remember. A darker ring on the outer edge, Caribbean blue with a couple of sunny spots, almost gray around the pupil. Framed by dark eyelashes—and that damned bruise on one eye.

Right. He said something. I should say something back. "He threw me under the bus. You qualify that as nice?"

Yes, my blush is flaring up, because I just agreed that my brother was trying to set us up, and he'd only do that if he knew I had feelings for the guy, but I don't even care anymore. Embarrassment is apparently my new normal when Thomas in the vicinity.

He chuckles. I can feel the vibrations in our still-joined hands. "Not liking the immediate result doesn't necessarily mean you won't like the final product."

I arch an eyebrow. "Is that what you tell your clients?"

This time he laughs outright. The sound echoes off the walls of the surrounding buildings and I could swear it makes the lights in the oak tree sway a little extra. Or maybe *I'm* swaying.

"Touché," he says. "Maybe you could give me a run for my money in repartee, huh?" He turns to frown toward the bar, where his friend and Simon disappeared. "Those two didn't know each other before this, right? We weren't set up to *that* degree? No, I saw your brother's face when he used the restroom. He was definitely surprised."

"I *knew* he didn't actually want me to see the restroom!" I accidentally squeeze Thomas's hand, and his strong hands squeeze right back. I think my heart skips a beat.

"Believe me," Thomas says, his eyes glinting behind his glasses. "You do not want to see that restroom. It's enough to make a guy stop drinking beer."

I turn my head to eye the rickety door suspiciously. "That bad?"

He nods. "That bad. I've been *once*, and this is one of my favorite bars in Toulouse."

As a comfortable silence settles, and the quiet conversations from the neighboring tables drift over, the lights from the tree flickers, a server brings a pink drink with a straw to each of the three women who grumbled at me earlier, and I wonder what the hell I'm doing.

Am I really sitting here, holding hands with a guy who's practically a stranger? I'm not even separated yet. I've barely managed to make sure Pierre knows I'm really leaving him without actually needing to talk to him directly.

Turns out he *did* notice on Monday night when I wasn't there for dinner, and no, he hadn't caught on before that. Guess if I needed a confirmation that my marriage was no good, that's as good a proof as any.

He tried calling me, the first time at about six, when I should have been there to start preparing dinner. Then again fifteen minutes later, and then every five minutes until I caved. Of course, I couldn't face the idea of talking to him myself—I need to be absolutely sure I won't cave and run back to him in England before I do that—so I handed my phone over to Simon and got him to explain things.

I could hear Pierre's yelling from across the room. Voice tinny through the phone but still easily recognizable. Simon kept his smile and held the phone away from his ear to keep from going deaf, while calmly explaining that we were getting separated and that he should expect paperwork to sign in a few days at most.

Simon didn't give me the details of what my husband yelled and that's probably for the best.

And that's the state of my life right now. I don't have room for another guy to come and swoop right in and sweep me off my feet. The chances of me falling on my ass are simply too high, and I'm not entirely convinced I'd be able to get back up. Even though Thomas's obvious interest makes me feel all warm and cuddly inside, I just don't…quite believe it.

What exactly is it that he likes about me? How can he know anything about me when *I* don't even know who I am first?

I need to figure that out before I even think about flirting with anyone.

And I need to prove to myself—and Pierre—that I can make it on my own. That was always the underlying threat with Pierre. That I needed him, that I would be lost without him.

Well, if I start leaning on someone else the minute I'm away from Pierre, I'm just proving him right.

So although I know I'm going to miss the physical contact, I gently extract my hand from Thomas's.

"Did I do something wrong?" Thomas asks.

I shove both hands into the pockets of my jacket so I won't be tempted to burrow back into the cocoon. "No, of course not. I just…" I sigh and slide a little lower on my chair. "My life's a mess right now. And I need to be the one to clean it up."

Thomas is leaning his elbows on his knees, hands loosely folded, as he looks up at me with those fascinating blue eyes and a soft smile. "I understand." He glances at our empty glasses on the tabletop. "How about another drink? No hand-holding, I promise. Just the chance to chat a little now that the black eye and the overly helpful wingmen are out of the way. Your brother will expect to pick you up here when they've had their pizza, right?"

Some sort of indie pop has started up, coming out of an ancient-looking loudspeaker stuffed into the far corner of the back yard, and the hum of conversation has picked up a little as people make themselves heard over the music. It all feels very safe, and secluded, and cozy.

I realize I *would* like to stay a little longer.

"I guess I could stay for one drink," I say. "Although it would serve Simon right if I just disappeared on him. You could be a serial killer for all he knows."

That soft chuckle again. "I'm not, I promise. But I'm not above joining in on a prank to teach your brother a lesson." He glances at me out of the corner of his eye. "He's not in the habit of punching people without good reason, right?"

I should have felt guilt. Sad. *Something* negative that he's bringing up me punching him yet again.

And yet, I start laughing. I laugh so hard, tears spring to my eyes and pour down my cheeks. I do that charming wheezing thing where you can't get enough air in because you're laughing too hard.

Thomas looks worried at first.

Then he joins in.

"You know what," he says when we finally start to calm down. "I don't even care if he punches me. You're worth the risk."

THIRTEEN

Pink Drinks With Umbrellas

Thomas

I CAN'T BELIEVE I just said that.

A woman turns me down—in the nicest way possible, yes, but it's still a rejection—and I go on to tell her I'm ready to be punched by her rugby-sized brother for the pleasure of hanging out with her?

It's a good thing Vincent isn't here anymore. He has enough ammunition for our next meeting with our college buddies as it is.

Still, it's true. Now, don't get me wrong. If I can avoid getting punched by the mountain of muscles, I will. But I *really* want to have a drink with Isabelle, get to know her better. There's something about her that speaks to me, on a deep level. Somewhere in the middle of my chest, if I'm not mistaken.

"I didn't even know you could get milkshakes here," I say while Isabelle wipes her cheeks, wincing when she realizes all those laughing tears have messed up her mascara.

"They're not on the menu." She eyes the door to the restroom behind her but must decide to trust my judgment on that subject and stays seated. "But if you ask for one, they'll whip one up for you."

I narrow my eyes. "I thought you came back to town less than a week ago. How did you know that?"

Her smile lights up her entire face and she huddles further into her coat with a contented sigh. "I noticed someone eating ice cream when we came in. If they have that, they should have all the necessary ingredients for it." She shrugs. "Ask nicely, and it's amazing the things you can get."

Her gaze turns unfocused and her smile falls. Probably thinking of times when asking nicely didn't do the trick.

"Well," I say quickly, to get her mind back to the present. "I can tell I'm in the presence of a real milkshake connoisseur. Do you want another milkshake, then? One of those pink drinks with umbrellas?"

The disdainful look she shoots at the three women with the pink drinks answers that question. "I'll have a Pastis, please."

I can't help it, my eyebrows shoot up. The anise-flavored liquor isn't exactly the drink I'd think of first for a woman. Except the few women I did hang out with when I was in college *did* drink all the same liquors as the guys, so I guess that prejudice is rooted further back in my past.

Luckily, Isabelle doesn't seem to take offense. "They don't have Pastis in England. I miss it. For some reason, it was the drink of choice in my friend group when I was in high school, so the nostalgia factor is strong."

"Nostalgia drink coming right up, then." I wave over a waiter and order two Pastis. While we wait for him to come back, we sit in silence, a comfortable one. I pretend to people-watch, but I keep stealing glances at Isabelle, discovering new details every time.

Like the way the blue lights from the tree sometimes reflect in her hair making her look like something out of a fairy tale. It looks like smooth silk and I'm dying to run my fingers through it to put my theory to the test. Or the way only the left side of her mouth twitches upward when she sees something she finds funny.

The third time I chance a glance in her direction, our gazes lock. Busted.

But I'm not the only one blushing.

"So are you from Toulouse?" she asks. I think she's trying to talk over her embarrassment and that's just fine with me.

"No, I grew up in Biarritz," I reply. "But I came here to study when I was eighteen, so I think I'm closing in on the status of adopted, at least. I lived close to campus in the Rangueil neighborhood while I studied, then moved to my apartment in Jolimont when I started working. I've lived in Toulouse for almost sixteen years."

The waiter comes back with our drinks; two high glasses with a dose of Pastis and two ice cubes each, and a mug of water to share. I hold up the mug, silently asking how much she wants.

"To the top." She chuckles. "Back in the day, we drank it almost pure, but I don't think I'm quite up for that anymore."

I fill her up and her Pastis turns from a translucent golden to a milky yellow. When her glass is full, it's almost white. I only pour a small amount into my own glass. I *do* like it this way, but I'm also aware of wanting to impress her. Apparently, any way I can, because being able to drink a Pastis with less water than Pastis isn't *that* much of a challenge.

When we've both had a sip, it's my turn for a small talk question. "I assume you did grow up in Toulouse?"

"Yes." Her eyes close in bliss as she swallows her first sip of Pastis. She must have been serious about missing it. "I'm afraid I don't have the accent—that would be too plebeian for my parents."

"I see. Playing right into the reputation of the Busca neighborhood."

One delicate cocked eyebrow. "You can say that again."

"So did you leave because you had somewhere else you wanted to be, or because you needed to be anywhere else but here?" I apply a healthy dose of humor to my tone, giving her the option of making a joke of her answer. It's the kind of question that can easily touch on some rather sensitive buttons.

She takes another sip as she studies me. I think she might not answer at all, until she does. "I left because I couldn't stand the thought of living so close to my parents anymore."

"Studying something that forces you to leave town is a good way of doing that without offending anyone."

She looks at me out of the corner of her eye. "You sound like you speak from experience."

I cock my head from side to side. "It's not really the same, though. There aren't all that many universities in Biarritz. Choosing something that I couldn't stay home for wasn't hard. Finding something to *stay* for would have been complicated." I take another sip of my drink and revel in the strong taste of anise and the burn of alcohol as it slides down my throat. "And I wasn't running away from my parents. I needed new friends." That last is said while intently studying the contents of my drink.

Isabelle nods. I'm not sure if she understand what I've left unsaid or if she simply knows I won't go into more detail. "Vincent seems like a nice friend. When he isn't dumping you in a bar to go have pizza with my brother, that is."

"He is. And he's actually a friend from high school. He was the only one worth keeping and I was thrilled when we were both accepted to schools here in Toulouse."

Silence settles around us again. It's comfortable.

Somehow, telling her about high school wasn't so scary. I'm aware that "telling her" is kind of a strong word for what happened, but it's infinitely more than I've ever told anybody else. Vincent knows—because he was there and suffered through much the same thing—but nobody else does.

Why would I want to tell my friends or colleagues about how much of a loser I was in high school? I'd rather build up an image of the Thomas I want to be, and let them see only that. High school Thomas died at graduation.

But it felt okay to tell Isabelle. I'm not sure if it is because she's virtually a stranger who I probably won't meet again after tonight, because she's a good listener, or because she has already told me about her secrets, her horror story, and I know she understands.

My secret is safe with her.

For the next half hour, we stick with small talk. Isabelle tells me some funny stories about the cultural shocks of a French person living in England. I tell her stories about my nerdiest friends and colleagues, the ones who play right into the stereotype of the socially inept computer geek who understands machines better than humans.

When the waiter comes to collect our empty glasses, Isabelle straightens in her chair. "I should probably find Simon and go home. I have about a hundred administrative papers to fill in tomorrow and on Sunday, to be ready to file them bright and early Monday morning."

I wince in sympathy. "Lots of paperwork for the separation?"

Isabelle groans. "If there's one thing I *didn't* miss from France, it's the paperwork. We got married here, though, and we're both French, so the paperwork would have been inevitable no matter where I was." She leaves enough to cover for her drink on the table, and I realize I'm too late to actually *buy* her a drink.

Not wanting to get into a stupid fight about it, I add in enough cash to pay for my own and leave it at that.

If the way she lifts her chin when she gets up is anything to go by, I'd say I just scored a point.

I stand up, too, and follow her across the yard and toward the bar. I don't want this night to end. So I take a chance. "I know you don't need a guy to protect you going home or anything, but would you mind if I accompanied you at least part of the way? I could do with a little walk, and I'll have to wait until Vincent is done with your brother before leaving anyway. He *does* need someone to walk him home."

I'm babbling, and the guy behind the bar gives me a pitying look as we walk past. I don't even care. I don't want to say goodbye to Isabelle yet, and I *still* don't have her number.

Out on the street, Isabelle dons a black beret-like cap and pulls up the collar of her coat. She looks like the epitome of French beauty as she leans back to look up at the swaying canopy of bare plane trees above us. The majestic trees line the avenue of La Lanterne Bleue from one end to the other. The numerous cars that usually hurry through here during rush hour have to squeeze into two narrow lanes because of the plane trees. First come, first served, seems to be the way things work in Toulouse.

"It's going to rain," Isabelle says. "And sooner rather than later. You sure you want to lose precious time to walk me home like we're in some old American movie?"

"Hey," I say, keeping my tone light. "I'll have you know I've walked lots of women home after a night out. And…not in the way that sounds. Ugh. Besides, I just told you, Vincent does need to be walked home. I do it all the time." Also, old American movies tend to end on a good-night kiss, right?

The smile she sends my way is soft and sweet, and totally at odds with the sarcasm in her words. "You certainly know how to make a woman feel special, Thomas."

Since I have no idea if I wanted to make her feel special or *not* to feel special, I opt to keep my mouth shut. And even though, judging by the loaded feel of the air and the wind blowing through the treetops, she is right about the coming rain, one thing is for certain: I *do* want to walk her home.

Anything to spend a few extra minutes with her.

"Let's give your brother a scare, shall we? How about I walk you home, then text Vincent to come get me at your address?"

FOURTEEN

Smiling, Soft-Looking Lips

Isabelle

THOMAS'S PLAN WORKS like a charm.

Not five minutes after he sends off a text to his friend, I spot Simon's large form hurrying down the street, Vincent with his bobbing red pom-pom beanie next to him. When Simon sees the two of us huddled together under the tiny overhang by the front door to stay out of the rain without going inside, he shakes his head and his look promises retribution.

I don't even care. I'm having too much fun.

I was right about the rainstorm coming. The first drop fell on my nose not three minutes after we left the bar, and by the time we reached my parents' street, it was already up to a drizzle. Now, ten minutes later, it's *pouring*. It shouldn't last long—it never does in Toulouse—but Simon clearly wasn't ready to wait for it to pass before checking up on me and figuring out why Thomas was at our house.

Serves him right for abandoning me with Thomas in the first place.

And I appreciate that he worries for me. At least someone cares about me.

When Simon and Vincent squeeze under the overhang with us, it gets decidedly crowded. I enjoyed waiting there with Thomas, under forced proximity, but not *too* close.

This is too close.

I have Simon on one side, his chest making up a wall of muscles at my eye level, and Thomas suddenly *very* close on the other side, now that Vincent has made room for himself on the far end. Thomas isn't as tall as Simon, so I'm faced with his chin.

It's a nice chin. With dark stubble. And smiling, soft-looking lips.

Eyes up!

I stare right into Thomas's blue eyes. His glasses offer a slight separation, since he still hasn't wiped off the rain they accumulated on our way here, but it's not enough to give the impression of distance.

I can smell his aftershave—I couldn't even begin to describe it, apart from noting it's not the same as Pierre wears, which is the only thing that matters, really—and the Pastis from earlier.

As my heart hammers in my chest, I search for something to say to ease up on the tension, but of course, I come up empty. My mind's a complete blank, all thoughts replaced with a set of clear blue eyes, and soft lips surrounded by stubble.

Thomas's friend comes to the rescue. "This is kind of a weird place to hang out. You guys realize that, right? There's, like, four of us on what feels like less than one square meter."

"Remember how I told you I live with my parents right now?" Simon's voice rumbles through my body—I've apparently plastered myself to him in an attempt *not* to plaster myself to

Thomas. "Well, so does Isa, and this is our parents' house. And we're *not* inviting you in for a digestif."

"Your parents do realize you're adults?"

"The jury's still out on that one, unfortunately. And in the meantime, we're going to keep behaving like teenagers out after curfew. So, keep your voices down, it was very nice to meet you, but please be on your way now."

All of this is delivered with a smile and a healthy dose of self-deprecation but Thomas and Vincent seem to get that the message isn't a joke.

"It's pouring," Thomas says. Not a complaint, simply an observation. Checking that we're really kicking them out in the middle of a rainstorm.

When Simon shrugs, my shoulder moves with his, and I end up mimicking his movement. A twitch of Thomas's lips—he must find it funny.

"You can stay here on the doorstep until it calms down if you want," I say. "Just make sure you don't make too much noise, please?" It's the best I can offer—because Simon is right, there is no way in hell we're inviting strangers inside at this time of night—and I'm proud to discover my voice is working correctly. I even got the cheeky tone right.

Thomas's lips break into a full-fledged smile, crooked tooth and all. If I can see only his mouth and not his face as a whole, we're *too close*. "How very kind of you, Mademoiselle," he says. "I'll be sure to remember your kind hospitality if our roles are ever reversed."

I nod regally, wondering what has gotten into me, and turn to unlock the front door. Once it's unlocked, but before opening the door, I meet Thomas's gaze. "I'm happy we ran into you tonight. I had fun."

"Me too," he replies easily. And before I can register what's happening, he's leaning in. If ever I needed a proof that I've been away from France for too long, this would be it.

Instead of understanding that he's leaning in to do *la bise*, the French kiss-on-the-cheek used to greet and say goodbye to someone, I think he's leaning in to kiss me. You know, for real. With my brother and his friend standing there watching.

So I throw my head back to get out of range. Bounce right into Simon's shoulder. Which works as a trampoline.

And I head-butt Thomas in the nose.

FIFTEEN

I Told You It Was a Believable Story

Thomas

I THINK I'M bleeding.

My whole face is in pain, all pulsing out from the area around my nose, making my eyes water, my mouth work, my jaw flex. I might be groaning, but I'm not entirely sure if it's out loud. I lean against the front door because I don't like the way my head is spinning and gingerly bring a hand to my nose. It comes away red.

Yep, bleeding.

"Oh my God!" Isabelle is in my face instantly, patting my cheeks, approaching my nose with her fingers but pulling away at my wince. "I'm so sorry! I can't believe I did that! It wasn't on purpose, I swear!"

This time, I definitely groan. "Don't worry about it," I say. "I shouldn't have—"

"This wasn't your fault!" Now that my eyes can focus on the woman taking up my entire field of vision, I can see she's gone white as a sheet. Her eyes are wide with panic and her hands keep twitching in my direction as if she wants to do something to help but doesn't know what. "How were you supposed to know I've totally forgotten about *la bise* in my decade across the Channel? We're in bloody France. The French customs should apply! Simon," she practically wails as she hits her brother's large chest. "Why does this keep happening to me?"

"I'm gonna go with fate." Simon is perfectly unperturbed, both by my bloody nose and by his panicked sister. He meets Vincent's gaze over mine and Isabelle's heads. "See, I told you it was a believable story. They're doing it again."

Vincent steps out from our hiding spot and into the downpour, apparently to get a better look at me. His pom-pom is already drooping from the earlier sprint in the rain, so I guess this isn't going to change much. "My God, he really *is* that nice. How could I never have noticed? I've known him since we were sixteen!"

Simon laughs. "Nobody's that polite and nice with his buddies. Who'd want to hang out with him? I knew this one guy—"

The front door, the one I've been leaning my shoulder against, opens. Inward. Revealing a dark-haired woman.

It's all I have the time to observe before I'm falling.

Onto the woman.

I hear an "oh, shit" that's probably Simon, a "Maman!" from Isabelle, and a gleeful cackle that I recognize as Vincent.

Personally, I only have the time for a panicked intake of breath before I land on the woman. My already bleeding nose explodes in pain—again—as I face-plant into the woman's stomach. One arm smacks into the floor, adding another source of pain, while the other gets tangled between—oh, God—her legs.

As soon as I can figure out what side is up, I scramble away on all fours, seeing nothing because my eyes are watering, but not caring. I just need to get *away*.

Once I'm not in contact with anyone and can only feel the grain of the solid hardwood floor beneath my palms and knees, I stop. And try to remember how to breathe.

"Isabelle! Simon! *What* is going on?"

"Maman!" Isabelle. "What are you doing up at this hour? I thought you'd be—"

"I *was* in bed. Then I got *out* of bed when I thought a band of hooligans had settled in on our doorstep!"

"Maman!" Simon. "You can't go barging outside in your pajamas if you think there are hooligans out there! Have some care for your own safety."

"Help me up, Simon. Don't just stand there like a buffoon." The sternness in the woman's tone would have anyone rushing to follow orders and I'm somewhat reassured to realize that Simon is no exception.

I still can't see what's going on. I'm curled in on myself with my head between my elbows, my hands over the back of my head, protecting me from any additional attacks. My nose feels like it's at least doubled in size, there's no way I'm trying to breathe through it anytime soon, and I can't seem to figure out how to draw a proper breath. The smell and taste of blood is everywhere.

"*Who* are you?" The mother's voice is like a whip. My entire body spasms, trying to figure out where the next attack is coming from.

But the question wasn't for me, apparently. "I'm Vincent, Madame. Thomas's friend. I assure you I'm not in the habit of coming into people's houses without invitation, but I think my friend needs a hand. Do you mind?"

"Oh, my God, Thomas!" I don't know what Isabelle has been doing up until now, but it clearly wasn't worrying about me. A soft thunk to my right, possibly as she falls to her knees beside me, then a gentle touch between my shoulder blades.

I spasm and draw a sharp breath.

"Maybe let his friend take care of him." Simon's voice is closer now, and a lot softer. "Even though I'm sure he'll forgive you in no time, it might be best if you kept your distance until he's recovered."

Isabelle whimpers and I hear her scramble away. I'm both desperate for her to go, and for her to stay.

My head's a mess, and not just because it's bleeding.

"Dude." A hand on my left shoulder. Vincent. My shoulder twitches, but it's not as violent as before. "You're starting to worry me. Are you all right?"

I'm definitely not "all right." But I'm also probably not dying. Very carefully, I unfold my body, watery eyes checking for any sudden movements around me. I can't really see anything clearly—I think I've lost my glasses somewhere and the tears won't stop running—but all the differently colored blobs are mostly staying still.

For the first time ever, I'm grateful for Vincent and his red pom-pom—I can recognize the shape and color and be certain he's the one kneeling by my side.

"Ouch," he says when he sees my face. Or so I assume. "You should get used to drawing stares, I think. With the mark that's gonna leave, there's no way your face is back to normal in less than two weeks."

Male chuckles from behind me. "I'm not sure you're helping."

Vincent throws his hands in the air. "Well, *I* don't know what to do with a bloody nose! I've never been in a fight or participated in a sport involving contact in my life." He points at Simon. "But *you* have. You're the rugby player. What's he supposed to do with this?"

"Oh, God." Isabelle's voice is weak and kind of tinny. I don't know if that's because of her or because my ears are still ringing. "Is his nose broken? Simon, please tell me his nose isn't broken."

"You want me to just tell you that or do you want me to actually check and then tell you the truth?"

Weirdly enough, Simon's irreverence and complete lack of panic calms me down. If I'd been in danger of dying or losing an eye or something, surely he would have taken the situation a little more seriously?

"The truth, idiot! Please, just…check on him?"

"Sure thing, Isa." A second, larger man-shaped form kneels down next to Vincent. My eyes must be clearing up a little, because I can almost make out his features. I can definitely tell the difference between Simon and Vincent, even without the pop-pom beacon.

"Let me see. I promise, I won't hurt you…much." Simon's large hands come up to gently probe my cheekbones, my forehead, my nose. That last makes we wince, but it's not too bad. The worst seems to be over.

"It's not crooked," Simon says. "Might be broken but I think it's the kind that'll heal itself in about three weeks. But you should put something cold on it. And it's still going to give you at least one shiner by tomorrow, possibly two. On top of the one you already have going!" The glee in that last statement makes me laugh for some reason.

"Are you still not going to explain to your colleagues how

you messed up your face?" Vincent asks. He's coming into focus enough for me to recognize his shit-eating grin.

"I haven't really thought that far out yet, Vincent." I blink furiously, trying to see the room clearly enough to search for my glasses. "My priority right now is getting home and putting something cold on my face."

"But if you live in Jolimont, that's going to add another thirty minutes, at least." Ah, the hand-wringing shape on the left is Isabelle, which means the other one, who is eerily similar when I can't make out much more than the shape, must be the mother. "Maman, I'm sure you have something in the freezer we can give him, right?"

The mother looks down at herself—eyesight clear enough to make out a large red stain on her beige pajamas, awesome—then sighs. "I assume these are friends of yours? We do not have a couple of perfect strangers bleeding all over our living room floor?"

"I'm not bleeding anywhere," Vincent says.

"Yes, they're friends," Simon says at the same time as Isabelle says, "We just met them at the bar."

I've had it with dealing with this situation half-blind. The fuzziness of what I'm seeing right now is mostly due to my bad eyesight—I can see Vincent and Simon, who are very close, fairly well, but the women farther away are still blurry—so I need my glasses. I pat around on the floor searching for them, while squinting at various shapes that *could* be what I'm looking for.

"What are you— Oh, your glasses!" Isabelle jumps into motion, coming near enough for me to make out facial features. She's still way too pale, and her eyes are darting left and right at a scary speed as she looks for my glasses.

"Here they a— Oh, no! Not again!" Shoulders slumped in defeat, Isabelle picks something up from underneath a burgundy couch and holds it out to me.

They're not bent out of shape this time, but the left lens is broken. The optician isn't going to be able to fix this in two minutes.

Sighing, I put them on anyway. At least my right eye will be able to see something. I suppress a wince as I set the glasses on my nose. It's not that bad—not compared to the pain that's still pulsing through my entire face, anyway.

Finally, I can see clearly.

Vincent and Simon are both on their knees in front of me. My friend with a slight smile and a glint in his eye that doesn't bode well for me in the future. Isabelle's brother with a look that I'm tempted to qualify as respect. I guess he knows first hand what kind of pain I'm in right now.

Also on her knees, by the couch, Isabelle. Tears are forming in her eyes, but I think she's fighting valiantly to keep them from falling. If the tense way she's holding herself is anything to go by, I think it's more for her mother's benefit than for mine.

So I finally look up at Isabelle's mother. Despite the bloody pajamas, she holds herself regally. Back straight, chin up. Hair somehow immaculate and with a gray streak over her right ear. Her eyes, so much like Isabelle's in shape and color, hold nothing of her daughter's warmth.

"So," the mother says. "Friend or stranger you picked up in a bar? The first will get a bag of frozen peas. The second will not."

I want to go back to the fetal position with my head protected. Maybe if I take my glasses off, she won't see me?

SIXTEEN

He Can Have the Bag of Frozen Peas

Isabelle

As if this situation wasn't complicated enough, Maman has to come and add her two cents?

My first reaction is to run and hide. I don't want to face the consequences of hurting Thomas—again!—and I don't want to explain to Maman how we met these two men, or even how I met Thomas the first time. I want to hide in my room and wait until the yelling is done.

But I can't do that. That's what I would have done when I was a teenager, when I didn't know how to stand up to my mother. When I hadn't decided to take control of my own life and prove to everyone, myself included, that I could adult like the best of them.

So I take a deep breath, pull back my shoulders, and stand up to face Maman.

"Does it really matter if they're friends or strangers, Maman? This man is hurt and needs something as simple as something cold to put on his swelling face. Is that really too much to ask for?"

I hear an intake of breath from behind me, but can't turn around to see who it is. Simon should certainly be surprised to see me behaving like this—I don't know Thomas and Vincent well enough to know how well they know me.

"Of course he can have the bag of frozen peas," Maman replies in that tone that implies I just asked her a ridiculous question. As if *I'm* the one being unreasonable. "That's not the subject here, Isabelle."

Incredibly enough, I feel anger rising. "Oh, it isn't? Then why did you make it the subject? Saying Thomas can have the peas only if he's a friend? That *is* what you said?" I think my entire body is shaking. I've never talked back to my mother like this.

It feels good.

"Ah, he has a name, I see." Maman looks down at Thomas like an evil queen staring down at her subject. She always gets like this when someone tries to stand up to her, or disagree. It's the reason why Simon and I have always avoided getting into arguments with her—we know we can't win.

But right now, I don't even care.

How can I ever expect to win if I never join the fight?

"Of course he has a name, Maman! We wouldn't have brought him to our doorstep if we didn't know him at least a little. Even if I just picked him up at a bar, like you seem so opposed to, I would have demanded he give me a name before inviting him home. *To my parents' house.* Do you even realize how ridiculous that sounds?"

Maman glances out the window before looking back at me. It's her version of rolling her eyes. She's standing there, halfway between the living room and the kitchen, with the front door still wide open to the deluge on the dark street outside, every inch the queen despite being the only person in the room in pajamas. I've never seen this woman lose her composure, not once in the thirty-four years I've known her.

She's certainly not going to start today. "I agree that is ridiculous, Isabelle. But you are a grown woman and I don't know you as well as I used to, so I cannot know what you consider ridiculous and what is par for the course. From what you say, inviting a nameless stranger into my home is not something you would do. But from your actions, I take it inviting someone with a name but with a bloody nose is quite all right?" Her nose lifts even higher. "I will not condone fighting in my house, no matter what the justification."

I can *feel* Simon tensing behind me. That was a jab at him.

I also hear a soft groan and I think that might have been Thomas. The almost-whistle is probably Vincent.

God, what an impression we're making on them tonight.

I'm not going to let Maman get a free hit at Simon, though. "Simon didn't cause the bloody nose. I did."

Oh my God, it shuts her up. Her mouth closes so quickly, the clack of her teeth slamming together echoes through the room.

Enjoying that a little too much, I add, "And I'm the one who gave him the black eye, too, when I hit him on the plane on Sunday."

Okay, I should learn when to stop.

"You *hit* someone, Isabelle? Giving them a black eye? *And* a bloody nose? Can I at least assume you had a justifiable reason for this behavior?"

There's movement behind me. I think all three men are getting up. Can't say I blame them for wanting to get on a more level ground with my mother.

"Not really," I answer Maman. "On the plane, he surprised me when I was sleeping and me hitting him was mostly reflex." I can't believe how calmly I'm explaining this. It's a subject I've been torn up about all week, and that makes me into an apologizing mess every time I meet Thomas, and yet now, I'm telling the story to my mother as if clocking someone for waking you up is the most natural thing in the world.

"The bloody nose happened just now on the doorstep when we were saying goodbye. It was an accident but definitely my fault."

Thomas comes to stand next to me. His lower face and jacket are all bloody and he looks a little crazy with one of his lenses broken, but he's smiling gently. "I know you didn't do either of those on purpose, Isabelle. No hard feelings, I promise."

A slight huff comes from behind Thomas. Probably Vincent.

Simon takes up position on my left, with a hand on my shoulder for support. "See, Maman, he's not a hooligan. In fact, he's a *very* decent guy who doesn't hold a grudge against the woman who hit him. Twice."

"No, *he* certainly isn't the hooligan, is he?" The look Maman sends my way is so cold, I wish I could steal Vincent's beanie.

"Great, Maman," Simon says. "Excellent way of showing your daughter you support her."

I should be continuing this fight with my mother on my own, but I seem to have reached my limit for today. My voice is nowhere to be found. I once again thank my lucky stars for my brother.

Maman's laser gaze switches to Simon. "What would you have me do, Simon? Isabelle admitted to hitting this man twice over the course of a week. Apparently without reason—not that there *is* a justifiable reason for violence, ever. How, exactly, do I *support* my daughter on this subject?"

Simon's hand clenches down on my shoulder even harder as he prepares to go into battle for me.

Thomas beats him to it. "It's probably not my place," he says gently. "But I'd suggest hearing her out when all of you have calmed down. I'm the person who was wronged both times, and I assure you, I hold no grudge against your daughter. Would this not be an indication that what happened was, indeed, an accident?"

Maman doesn't have an immediate come-back—which is rare in and of itself. She always has an answer to everything.

The silence doesn't last long, though. "How do I know you don't claim to hold no grudge only to get what you want from my daughter? She's an attractive woman, in a vulnerable state right now. Some men would take advantage."

"Maman!" Simon roars.

I'd love to do the same, but I can't breathe, let alone talk.

Thomas clears his throat. Like we're at a polite dinner party and he has something to say. Somehow, it draws everyone's attention.

"I won't disagree on your daughter being attractive, Madame, but I must fervently disagree with the rest of your statement. Your daughter is far from vulnerable and can most decidedly stand up for herself. Also, I'm not the kind of man who would take advantage of a woman, or look to be the rebound for someone freshly separated."

Maman's eyebrow twitches. She didn't expect him to know about my *very* recent separation.

"On that note..." Thomas brushes down the front of his jacket as if he'd picked up a lot of dirt on Maman's immaculate floors, discovers the drying blood, and winces. "I think it's about time Vincent and I took off."

He turns to face me and I focus on the one eye that's easily visible behind his glasses, doing my best *not* to stare at the bloody state of his nose. "I had a lovely evening, Isabelle. I was glad to see coming home has been good for you."

"Thank you," I whisper. "And again, I'm *so*—"

"—Sorry to have hit me. Yes, I know." When he smiles, I can see blood on several of his teeth, including the crooked one, and my heart breaks a little.

A quick nod, and he grabs his friend's arm and pulls him toward the front door.

Serves Maman right that he doesn't even acknowledge her.

Simon rushes after the two men, to shake their hands before they leave. When he closes the door behind them, he spares one dirty look for Maman before ushering me toward the stairs.

"Come on, Isa. Let's get you ready for bed. You have to tell me *all* about your *date* with Thomas."

I'm about to contradict him. It wasn't a date. We just had a drink and hardly talked. Until I see my mother's face. "That sounds great, Simon." And even though my mother clearly expects a debrief, I brush right past her. "Let me tell you all about my *date*."

SEVENTEEN

What the Hell's the Difference Between Indigo and Violet?

Thomas

IT'S ONLY BEEN ten days, but the sheet of paper I'm fiddling with is already frayed at the edges. I was about five seconds from throwing it in the wash with my jeans this weekend and the panic I felt was nothing short of pathetic.

It's the ripped-off corner of a pizza menu, from the pizza place Vincent and Simon went to when they abandoned Isabelle and me at the bar that fateful Friday night. Down the side, in the only available white space, Simon has written his name and phone number, and the comment, "I can't give you *her* number, but here's mine. Just in case." He slipped it into my hand when I left their house, like some slick mafioso in a movie.

Is it weird that I'm obsessing over a *guy's* phone number?

What am I supposed to do with this, anyway? Text him to ask for news of his sister? Talk about awkward. Maybe he wanted news on my physical state? Make sure I didn't have any lasting after-effects from the broken nose?

I'm *not* going to send the guy a selfie.

And yes, my face is every color of the rainbow right now. The first bruise is down to a faded, sickly yellow. It would hardly have been noticeable if that had been the only one. Which is isn't, of course. I have a mostly black line running over my nose and halfway across my cheekbones. The nose itself is the kind of red you associate with old drunkards.

All in all, I look like I was in a fight, and lost.

As I glance up from my desk, I catch three colleagues staring at me before they avert their eyes, pretending they've just been staring into space while thinking. I share an office space with my team, all ten of them. I have the "corner office," which allows me the luxury of not having anyone behind me *and* a spot by a window, but that's about everything that sets me apart from the others. We all have the same basic desks, with a tiny cabinet on wheels for our personal things, the same blue-backed office chairs, and the same laptops and double monitors.

Anita, the only woman on the team, has been awarded the other corner seat opposite me, and she has been sending me weird looks ever since I came in with the first shiner. I can't quite decide if she's morbidly fascinated by my discolored face or if she's worried I'm secretly a serial killer and she'll be my next victim. Her eyes are glued on me *every* time I look up. And despite being caught, she never looks away for more than five minutes. It's a wonder she's getting anything done, honestly. And yes, I checked. She *is* producing code, as efficiently as before.

The reactions from the guys on the team range from *couldn't care less* to *I must know what happened or I won't get a moment of sleep.* Benjamin and Clément are in that last category.

I'm starting to wonder if I should have just told them the truth from the beginning. Maybe then I wouldn't be pestered *all the time.*

"The power went out and you walked into a door." Clément. Here we go again.

"You approached an old lady on the street and she knocked you down with her purse." Benjamin.

"You're part of a fighting ring, and for the first time, you lost. Well, second now."

"You went on a date and instead of getting a kiss, she knocked you flat."

Shoving the paper with Simon's phone number into my pocket, I throw a death glare at Clément and Benjamin. "Do I have to separate you two, like you're kids in school? Will that get you to focus on doing your jobs?"

That shuts them up—for now.

Anita narrows her eyes at me from across the room. I ignore her.

I'm supposed to be looking at the stats from our latest app. See which functions are being used, where people are leaving comments, which profile types are the most frequent users, that kind of thing. But after staring at the numbers for a couple of minutes, none of them make any sense, and I realize I'm once again fiddling with the torn-off pizza menu.

Clearly, I'm not going to get anything done before I do something about this.

I enter the number into my phone, and without thinking too much, send off a quick message.

Thomas: *Hi, Thomas here.*

Yeah, "quick" pretty much sums it up. I want to ask about Isabelle, but can't bring myself to actually do it. I *could* give an update on my bruises, but maybe he doesn't care, and would that make me look self-centered?

Now that I'm looking at the message on my screen, I feel ridiculous. Who waits for ten days, and then sends of a message with nothing but a greeting?

My phone vibrates with a message.

Simon: *Hi, Simon here.*

Great. He's making fun of me.

My hand makes it halfway to my face before I remember how much a face-palm hurts these days. Yes, I learned that the hard way. Several times over.

Okay, never mind. I sent the message, he replied. End of story. If he had any important information to give me, he would have. He doesn't. End. Of. Story.

Simon: *Good to see you're still alive, dude. How's the nose? Missing any colors of the rainbow?*

Only when Anita's frown deepens do I realize I'm smiling.

Thomas: *Let me see. I got blue, violet, black (but that isn't even part of the rainbow, is it?), green, yellow, red… I don't think any of this qualifies as orange. I feel like I'm missing a color?*

I send off the message and put down my phone. My chest feeling a lot lighter suddenly, the numbers on my screen start making sense. Only fifty new downloads this week. Not bad for a new app, but hardly enough to make it profitable for our company. I sigh as I look at the next graph. Especially when twenty of them uninstalled it within two days.

My phone vibrates.

Simon: *Dude, you made me google the colors of the rainbow. Not cool. And what the hell's the difference between indigo and violet?*

This time I snort, which makes me wince, and everyone else turn in my direction.

I pretend not to notice and school my face into a serious mask as I feign studying the numbers on my monitor.

Hey, at least one user seems to like the app. A woman in the age range thirty to fifty has used the app several times a day for the last seven days. She even left the app a rating—only three stars, but still.

I click on the review to see what she has to say.

A good start. *The interface is beautiful and easy to use. I love how the app indicates all places where art can be found, but I'd have preferred to easily differentiate between museums, art galleries, and private estates that are only open to the public once a year. More details on the exhibitions would also have been great. Right now, the descriptions aren't enough to let me really understand what I'll get if I visit.*

Well. Not so bad, I guess. And it's certainly constructive.

That part on having different categories shouldn't be difficult to do. We can probably use the same logic as when we tag a recipe as a starter, a main dish, or a dessert.

I click open our idea board and type in the info. I assign it to Anita, for one because she's staring at me *again*, and two because she's the one who did the tagging in the recipe app, so she should be able to produce the code in mere hours.

Glancing at my phone lying on my desk with its unanswered message, I get an idea. I lock my session on the laptop, grab my phone, and make a beeline for the restroom. Once inside, I lock the door and open the front camera on my phone.

If I turn my face just so under the restroom lights... I snap a picture. Quickly, I edit in two circles, one under my left eye, the other closer to my nose on the right.

> **Thomas:** *I think the part under my eye is indigo, whereas the other highlighted area is closer to violet. If needed, I can get one of my graphic designers to confirm.*

I attach the photo and hit "Send."

I'm not even back to my desk when the reply comes back, bringing another smile to my face. And yes, it does make Anita frown.

> **Simon:** *Ah, thank you for clearing that up for me. I'll make sure to keep the photo for future reference. Already got new glasses, I see?*

I lock into my laptop and check out a few more stats before replying. After all, I am the manager and have to set a good example for the team. I can't spend all day on my phone like some teenager. When I've created three more idea tickets for the team based on what I can glean from the numbers, I type in a reply to Simon.

> **Thomas:** *I should get my glasses back from the optician by Friday. These are my old ones. I've been nearsighted for long enough to have a fair supply of backups.*

> **Simon:** *Ah, I see. I showed the picture to Isa and she confirms those are a bit dated, fashion-wise. I wouldn't know. But she's happy you're not walking around half-blind because of her.*

My heart has suddenly decided to make itself known. It feels like it's training to run a marathon. Or at least enlarging my ribcage.

He showed the picture of my bruised face to Isabelle?

I want to reply. Something witty, something nice, *anything*. But knowing Isabelle might read it, I can't find a single thing to write.

> **Simon:** *Isa got your tongue, dude? Don't worry, I didn't show the messages, only the picture. By the way, this Sunday is the first Sunday of the month, which means free admittance to museums. I'm taking Isa to the Museum of Natural History after lunch. Just saying.*

I stare at that message for so long, my laptop's screen saver activates.

Did he just invite me to "bump into" Isabelle on Sunday? Does she know? Would she *want* to bump into me? What state will my face be in by then?

What do I do?

EIGHTEEN

Oh, Look Who's Here

Isabelle

EVERY FIRST SUNDAY of the month, all the permanent exhibits of the museums in Toulouse are free. It's something Simon and I always try to take advantage of when we're in the city together. It allows us to discover new museums, or to revisit old favorites, without spending a euro. Since we're far from the only ones taking advantage of this arrangement, it's also an excellent chance for people-watching. If you want to enjoy the exhibits in silence by yourself, you're out of luck, but if you enjoy watching people as much as you enjoy the paintings, it's the perfect situation.

Today we're doing an old classic: the Museum of Natural History. We went often when we were kids, but then it closed for renovation for several years, and I haven't been back since. I've heard lots of great things about it, so I'm looking forward to our little outing.

I've been home for three weeks now. All the paperwork for the separation is signed, I have my own bank accounts and have retrieved my half of our money. I've officially resigned from my job without too much yelling, and Pierre seems to have accepted the situation.

The first week he called me at least ten times per day. I never answered, only let Simon field some of the calls for me from time to time, to check that Pierre didn't need to tell me something important. He never did.

The second week, he called only once a day, usually when he came home from the office—which is apparently even later than what he used to do, closer to midnight most nights. When he got a grumpy Simon for the second time, he made sure to make his calls earlier in the day.

This week, he has only tried to call me twice. I let them both go to voice mail.

One of these days I'll have to actually talk to him, but I'm not quite there yet. Soon.

Today, I'm going to check out the wall of skeletons. The pictures on the museum's website look awesome. I can't wait to see it.

We're approaching the Museum on the allées Jules Guesde. Like the museum, the large avenue has been redone in recent years, reducing the space taken up by cars to only two small lanes on the left, leaving a huge lawn lined with young-ish plane trees straight down the middle with room for kids and dogs to run and tumble, a large sidewalk on the right-hand side for pedestrians, *and* a bicycle lane for bikes. It's rare to have so much open space without fear of being run down by a car in the center of a city like Toulouse, and it brings a smile to my face every time I see it.

The line to enter the Museum starts ten meters down the avenue. Inside the arched entrance to the park Jardin des Plantes where the museum is located, the line continues for about fifty meters up to the main entrance.

No matter. I'm with my brother and we have all the time in the world.

"So." I nudge Simon with an elbow because I can't be bothered to take my hands out of my nice and warm pockets. Toulouse doesn't get very cold in winter, but close enough that fog is forming in front of my mouth when I talk, and for me to wear my trusted beret every time I go out. "When are you going to tell me why you're living with the parents? I thought you were happy in Perpignan?"

"I was." Simon isn't meeting my eyes, stretching his neck to look at all the people in front of us in the queue. "Then I wasn't, so I came home."

"Thank you so much for that detailed explanation. Everything is perfectly clear now."

"That's all you're getting for now, Isa." He bumps me back, making me fly halfway across the sidewalk. "But I promise, once things clear up a little, you'll be the first I'll talk to."

I frown up at Simon, wondering what put that touch of doubt in his eyes. Oddly enough, wondering if the fact that he's letting his hair grow for the first time since he was ten somehow has anything to do with what's bothering him. "You're kind of worrying me," I tell him honestly. "I'm leaning on you so heavily right now, and you're dealing with whatever shit has happened all by yourself. I don't want to put too much pressure on you."

The smile he gives me is sincere, and it reaches his eyes. "Your mess of a life doesn't put any extra pressure on me, Isa. Never fear. In fact, you're a great source of fun and laughs, believe it or not."

"You think my life is fun—"

"Oh, look who's here!" Simon starts waving like a five-year-old who sees his grandpa for the first time in months. It seems to be directed at two men coming through the arch. One of them has a red pom-pom beanie...

"Vincent! Thomas! Imagine running into you here! You going to see the wall of skeletons too?"

There's something suspiciously cheery about Simon's reaction. It's like he was expecting to run into these two—but how could that be possible?

Wait.

He showed me that selfie of Thomas, so he must have the number of at least one of the men. Probably Thomas himself.

How did that happen?

And what am I supposed to do now?

Vincent bounds over to shake hands with Simon. "Hey, good to see you again. How are you? Mother hasn't kicked you out of the house yet?" He takes a step toward me, then stops, his head slightly outstretched. "*La bise* okay?"

Great, he's worried I'm going to head-butt him. "Of course it's okay." I lean forward and we do *la bise*, kissing the air next to each other's cheeks, no forehead to nose or anything.

Vincent steps back, and in his place, Thomas smiles hesitantly.

He's got his glasses back, the ones with the metal frames. The ones I bent out of shape on the plane and broke one lens of two weeks ago. He's mostly free of the bruising now, although there's like a shadow on his right cheekbone, something I probably wouldn't even notice if I wasn't looking for it.

Three weeks since we first met and he's still carrying around the ghastly reminder of my clumsiness.

"Hi," I say stupidly. I lean forward to do *la bise*—I am getting this *right*, dammit—aiming for my left cheek against his left cheek. Except he seems to be doing the opposite.

Why? Why is this happening *now*? It's a classic issue when people from different regions meet, because everybody doesn't start the *bise* on the same cheek. It makes for funny situations when you're with friends. A lot less fun situations when you're in the workplace.

Or when you're greeting a guy you like who you already head-butted the last time he tried to do this with you.

We both draw up short. Except we're a lot closer than we were. I can feel his minty breath on my face and see the reflection of my surprised face in his glasses. Also, his lips are *right* in front of my eyes.

I can't seem to look anywhere else.

Simon, please help.

Sibling telepathy must be a thing. "Hah, attempting to add another bruise to the poor guy's collection, Isa? Let's do this together, shall we? Left cheek against left cheek. That's the way we do it in Toulouse, remember?"

My eyes are still locked on those soft-looking lips and the dark scruff surrounding them, but I see the blush rising in Thomas's cheeks. What does he have to be embarrassed about?

Maybe by the fact that I'm staring at his lips.

Forcing my gaze up to meet his oh-so blue eyes, I manage a smile and stretch my head *way* out right before approaching him.

"There we go," Simon says. "Greeting people like a proper *toulousaine*. We'll knock those English tendencies out of you in no time, Isa, you'll see."

The official greeting out of the way, I take one step away from Thomas in the hopes my brain will function again once I'm out of his personal space. Or rather, once he's out of mine.

I slap at Simon's arm. "I think we've had enough violence as it is, Simon. I'll be doing my transformation *peacefully* from now on, thank you very much."

Thomas roars with laughter, head flung back and hands on his belly.

"I'll agree to that," he says. His eyes flick from me, to Simon, to the queue inching forward toward the museum entrance. "So, uh, you're going to the museum?"

His awkwardness somehow puts me a little more at ease. With a smile, I look at the people in front of us in the queue, behind us, the Museum. "Looks like it, doesn't it? I'm mostly interested in the wall of skeletons for today. I haven't had a chance to see it since they renovated."

"Right." Thomas swallows. "I, uh… Okay, I'll have to own up to the fact that someone told me to check out the Museum because it's apparently good, but I have no idea what to expect. I thought there would be animals and stuff, but… A *wall* of skeletons?"

Simon has somehow managed to pull Vincent off to the side, showing him something on his phone. Giving us privacy. I don't know if it's intentional or accidental, but I'll take it.

"It does sound kind of morbid like that, doesn't it?" I smile up at Thomas, our eyes locking. "But it's quite normal for a museum of natural history, I assure you. They all usually have skeletons of different animals, right? Well, here, they've set them up in one of the museum's walls. If you can even call it that. There are windows on both sides, and they're set up as if in action, so it looks like they're running through the park outside, or swimming through the ocean. You'll see, it's awesome."

"You seem to know a lot about it for someone who hasn't lived here for over a decade." Without breaking eye contact, we move along under the arch and officially into the Jardin des Plantes as the queue inches forward.

I could stare into his blue eyes forever. Except I won't, because

I need to prove to myself that I can make it on my own. Which I will. I'll just enjoy this unexpected surprise while I can.

It's a bit like enjoying a good book or movie for a couple of hours. They allow you to take a little break from real life, dream of heroic actions and happily ever after, to help you make it through the not-so-romantic everyday life.

I'll be back to the boring and scary normal in no time.

Right now, I'm going to enjoy visiting a museum with a handsome man at my side.

NINETEEN

Big, and Kind, and Oddly Shaped

Thomas

ISABELLE BECOMES BEAUTIFULLY animated when she talks about the museum we're about to enter. Her dark eyes sparkle as she uses her entire body to explain to me why this wall of skeletons is so wonderful.

She could be talking about rotting cabbages for all I care, as long as I get to see her animated enthusiasm. Her black hair falls gently to her shoulders from beneath her beret, framing her pale face. I think she's wearing lipstick today, which is something I haven't seen on her before. I hope it's a sign she's feeling better.

Every time she thinks of something new to tell me about, like the human skeleton riding a horse skeleton, she touches my forearm. As if that is needed to draw my attention. I don't think I'd notice if Vincent and Simon started fighting. I'm not even entirely sure they're still with us. Couldn't care less.

Isabelle clearly isn't aware she's touching me, it's just her way of interacting with people she's talking to. I'm hyper-aware of every touch, and the minute we're through the doors to the museum and into the relative warmth of the reception hall, I remove my jacket to fold it over one arm. The one farthest from Isabelle.

She grabs onto my arm. "Oh, don't you just love the elephant? They're, like, my favorite animals, ever." Huge smile across her face, she looks up at the enormous elephant placed on a pedestal in the middle of the reception area. Its trunk is lifted like it's calling out to someone, and I have to admit I'm impressed by how alive and in-action it looks.

About a dozen kids are running around the elephant, pretending to shoot it, trying to jump up to touch its tail, stealing each other's sweets, screaming in fright/joy as they chase each other.

This might be why I've never come here before—too many kids. Although, I guess with the right company, a bunch of screaming kids in the background isn't such a big deal.

When Isabelle's eyes are back on mine, I return her smile. Her hand is still on my forearm and the warmth of her fingers is heating me up through the thin material of my sweater.

Yes, I *may* have put on the sweater my mother *swears* makes my eyes look good, a dark blue wool that's impossibly soft to the touch. Vincent mocked me when he saw it, but Isabelle doesn't seem to notice the effort I put into it—which would have been embarrassing—so I'll call that a win.

"What is it about elephants that you love so much?" I ask her.

She sighs happily. "They're big, and kind, and oddly shaped, and can eat peanuts with their trunks." She glances up at the giant above us. "They have a great sense of community and family. And they're *awesome*."

"Good enough. Awesome is always good."

"So what's your favorite animal, then?"

I'm brought up short by the fact that I don't know the answer to that question. I always had a favorite animal when I was a kid, but what adult goes around thinking about which animals are the best?

Isabelle is who.

"Weirdly enough," I tell her, "I'll have to think about that." We've reached the ticket counter and I get four entries to the permanent exhibition. We have to get tickets even though they're free. I hand them out—and yes, Vincent and Simon are still there, engrossed in a conversation that seems to be on the different kinds of cheeses to put on pizza—and we're through the turnstiles of the museum.

The first exhibits seem to be about stones, or lava, or something like that. I don't get the time to figure it out because I'm dragged through the dark hallways by Isabelle. It's not that she's pulling hard or anything, but instead of grabbing onto my clothed forearm, she has taken hold of my hand.

I'm not entirely sure what do to about this, especially when Simon notices and smirks. But I'm not about to pull away, so I just go with it. I let her lead me toward a room with more light.

The wall of skeletons.

The entire museum wall is made of glass, covering both floors of the building. There are actually *two* walls of glass. And in the space between the two, dozens, maybe hundreds, of skeletons are set up as if in action.

It's magical.

Isabelle draws to a stop, her mouth open in a wide smile as she stares up at the skeletons in front of us.

It's a man on a horse. And they're not standing still. The

horse is galloping, and the man is leaning over the horse's mane, holding on as they rush forward.

"That's amazing," I say.

"I know!" Isabelle jumps in place like a four-year-old about to get ice cream. The worried and scared woman I met three weeks ago is nowhere to be seen. She has been replaced by a wonderful woman who loves what she's seeing and not feeling an ounce of embarrassment for it.

She's still holding my hand.

I lift my head to try to understand the set of skeletons above the horse. "Are those two…doing it?" It's awesome that they've set the animals up as if they were alive and in action, but I'm a bit surprised they'd do something so…explicit.

Isabelle's peal of laughter draws the attention of a young couple next to us, and three kids who must be about six, stare up at Isabelle with huge smiles, wanting to know what the joke is.

"That's a gazelle and a lion. You see a lot of lions *doing* gazelles?"

Oh. The lion is attacking the gazelle from behind, her jaws frozen just before she bites down on her target's neck.

"That's so cute, he's blushing again." Simon, now on my left, leans forward to meet Isabelle's gaze on my right. "What'd you do this time?"

"*I* didn't do anything. Tell me, Simon, what do you think those two skeletons are doing?" She points to the hunting scene.

I don't turn to look at Simon. I don't need to. His laughter, and that of Vincent from right behind me, is quite enough.

And yet, I don't move.

Because Isabelle is still holding my hand.

"Did you see the hippopotamus?" Vincent says. "It's *huge*."

"Why don't you go check that out, then?" I tell him, not

bothering to hide my annoyance. "I'm sure Simon would love to see it, too."

Simon's still chuckling. "Nothing I'd love more. Show the way, friend." He seems to be *for* me holding his sister's hand, and getting rid of him so I can be alone with her. Is that weird behavior for a brother? I feel like it should be, but I wouldn't know since I never had any sisters. And I'm not going to question it.

Because I'm alone with Isabelle.

If being surrounded by dozens of screaming kids and tired parents qualifies as alone, of course.

Acutely aware that my hand is starting to sweat, I glance down at Isabelle. She's still looking at the skeleton horse while she chews on her lower lip. She seems to have worn off the lipstick already—and now I'm staring at her lips.

Will the parents freak out if I kiss a woman in front of their kids?

Surely not, if it's just a quick kiss.

"Which, uh…" Isabelle draws a shaky breath before trying again. "Which skeleton is your favorite?"

I'm a fraction of a second away from replying "yours," but luckily, I catch myself in time. Talk about coming off as creepy.

"I'll have to look at more of them before making up my mind." I tear my gaze away from her lips and focus on her brown eyes instead. "Considering what just happened, I don't dare say the lion."

The blush rising in Isabelle's cheeks must match my own. And thank God neither of our wingmen are here to witness this.

"You don't have a favorite animal and you don't have a favorite skeleton? I'm starting to seriously doubt your character, Thomas."

I love hearing my name coming through her lips. "Maybe I'm hesitating because there are too many animals to choose from. They're all awesome."

"Hmm." Isabelle narrows her eyes at me. "Now you're just saying things to please me. Not all animals are great. Take hyenas, for example."

"That's an odd example. There aren't many hyenas in France."

Isabelle starts pulling me along the glass wall, her eyes scanning the exhibit as if she suddenly finds it *extremely* interesting. "I *may* have watched the *Lion King* yesterday," she mumbles.

I give her hand a squeeze. "That explains it, I guess. Oh, what's this?" The skeleton of something that is the approximate size of a cat, but it's jumping, I think, apparently hunting something. And in place of hands or paws, it has… "It has spider legs instead of paws."

Isabelle laughs at my expression. "Those are its wings. It's a flying fox. A type of bat," she explains when my face must convey the fact that I have never heard of a fox that could fly before.

"That's just creepy."

"It kind of is. Which is what makes it awesome." She's so close to the glass, I'm worried she'll soon flatten her nose against it, like some of the younger kids we walked past earlier. She *is* like the kids, actually.

"You really enjoy this, don't you?"

"Why else would I come here?" She frowns. "Why would you go to the museum if you don't enjoy it?"

To get the chance to see you again.

"To learn things." It's the first thing that comes to mind. It's what I associate with museums. They have things to look at, with plaques giving lots of information about them. Learning. And so, so, dull.

Isabelle is cocking her head, studying me as if trying to understand some great secret. "Then why isn't there anything to learn in your museum app?"

There isn't anything to learn in our app? Well, of course not. That's what the museum is for. If you can learn everything from the app, why go to the museum at all?

I open my mouth to answer, then... "Wait. You've been using our app?"

TWENTY

Whales are Awesome

Isabelle

I SHOULDN'T HAVE said that.

Everything was going so well. I was enjoying the visit, I loved showing the skeletons to Thomas, felt safe in a large crowd of noisy people who couldn't care less what I was doing. I'm even holding Thomas's hand, and plan to continue to do so as long as I can pretend, even to myself, that it was all an accident.

It's so nice and innocent and sweet. Exactly what I need.

Except now Thomas is going to know I've been stalking his apps and he's going to think I'm weird.

"I may have downloaded a couple of them," I hedge.

Thomas flashes his crooked tooth. "A *couple*? So not just the museum one?"

I should tell him I got the museums app and the one with the recipes and leave it at that. So naturally, I blurt out, "I downloaded all of them."

Seriously, where is Simon when I need him?

Thomas doesn't seem to think it's weird, though. In fact, he looks genuinely happy. "So did you test all of them? Any favorites?"

We're kind of blocking the view of the horse skeleton for a family of six, so I pull Thomas along toward the taxidermy area. It's not as fascinating as the wall of skeletons, but the animals are in very good shape and often in funny positions, and the section they're in is dark and cozy—which sounds perfect right about now.

Vincent and Simon are in front of the hippopotamus skeleton, gesticulating and arguing over something. I don't bother signaling where we're taking off to.

"I've quite enjoyed the app with the recipes," I tell Thomas. "I had fun entering random ingredients from my mom's cupboards and seeing what it came up with. I ended up with a very tasty variant of chili con carne, and a rather odd cake with both carrots and bananas."

"I didn't even know that existed," Thomas says as he sidesteps a large woman who's too focused on her toddler to see where she's going.

"It's your app."

"Yes, well, we don't actually come up with the recipes. The point of the app is that it searches the web for suitable recipes for you. When you were following the recipe, you were actually on the web page of whoever posted the recipe and no longer in the app."

"Oh. Okay." I stop in front of the butterfly exhibit, my eyes drawn to a huge, sparkling blue specimen that has never lived on European soil. Its color is exactly like Thomas's eyes. Before

I can say that out loud, I say the next thing that comes to mind. "Couldn't you do the same things for the museums, then? Most places have a pretty detailed description of their exhibits on their homepage, as do travel guides, or even travel blogs."

I can't tell for sure since my eyes are still glued to the blue butterfly, but I think Thomas is narrowing his eyes at me. "Are you the one who left that review on the app? The one requesting categories and more information?"

He reads the reviews?

I hadn't expected that. Now I can't remember what I wrote. It wasn't all bad, was it? I was just so frustrated with the lack of information and when I got the pop-up asking me if I wanted to rate the application, I clicked yes.

"Uh…" I glance up at him to try to gauge his reaction. "Maybe?"

Instead of the anger I was fearing, he lights up with a huge smile. "That review was so helpful! The categories are already developed and will be tested next week. You should have your new feature by the next version, so, probably next Friday."

"Wow. That's quick."

"That's how we roll." He grins at the slick line, and it makes me laugh.

But it's a weird laugh. I'm not sure why, but I'm suddenly feeling all shaky. My heart rate has sped up, my hands are clammy, and I realize I'm mapping out the quickest way to the exit.

Why?

Thomas's hand squeezes mine and his smile drops. He noticed something's off. "What's wrong? Was it something I said?"

It wasn't, of course. Not something he said.

Something my brain somehow *expected* him to say. Something scathing and mean.

The kind of thing Pierre would have said.

When was the last time I criticized something Pierre did? I can't even remember. Because whenever I said something that could be interpreted as a criticism, he would take it as one. And retaliate. He'd find a weakness—and we'd been together for long enough for him to know *exactly* which buttons to push—burrow in, and do as much damage as possible.

I guess his tactic worked, because I stopped ever saying anything that could be taken in a negative manner. No more criticisms.

No more opinions.

Was this how I developed my habit of commenting on things online? A safe way to express my opinion without Pierre hounding me for it?

Now, don't get me wrong, I'm no troll. I don't go around searching for flaws and pointing them out. But I'll give anything an honest review, be it good or bad. And all the bad ones are turned in a constructive manner, explaining what I would have liked to see improved.

Which is exactly what I did for Thomas's app. I saw something that had a lot of potential, but fell short in certain areas.

Yet when I told him, he didn't freak out or say anything mean.

How could I not have realized I'd become this way? Why did I let Pierre scare me like this? And for so long!

"You're kind of freaking me out," Thomas whispers. "Do you need some fresh air? Your skin has turned so pale, I'm thinking back, trying to remember if I've ever seen you in direct sunlight."

His joke breaks me out of my spell and I manage a wobbly smile. "It's winter in Toulouse. You won't be seeing me, or anybody else, in direct sunlight for a while." People say the weather is bad in England, but winter in Toulouse is honestly depressing. Clouds, rain, and cold—but never any snow.

He smiles in acknowledgment of my lame joke, but it doesn't reach his eyes. He's genuinely worried.

"I'm fine," I assure him. "I just had a...flashback, I guess. It's nothing."

Realizing how sweaty my palm has become, I try to pull my hand out of his, but Thomas isn't having it. He entwines our fingers and gives me a squeeze. "Didn't really look like nothing," he says.

It wasn't, and I'll have to analyze what just happened later. When I'm home and alone. Not here and now and in front of Thomas and his piercing blue eyes.

Time for a distraction. I pull on his hand and rush us farther into the displays. "You have to come see the polar bear. It's amazing."

"Because it's large, and fluffy, and awesome?" Good, he's going to let it go.

"Exactly!"

We come to a stop in front of the polar bear and its buddies. Two boys who can't be more than four stand in front of us, noses and hands pressed to the glass.

"You know what else is awesome?" Thomas says.

I almost give myself whiplash when I snap around to look into his eyes. That tone... My heart suddenly beats furiously in my chest, both from happy anticipation of what he might say, and in abject fear of this moving way too fast for me.

"Whales," Thomas says. "They're also large and awesome. Not sure about the fluffy part. *That's* my favorite skeleton, by the way—there was one hanging above us but too large to go in the wall out there—*and* it's my favorite animal. See? Found it."

My emotions are all over the place and I have no idea what expression is on my face. Disappointment, surprise, joy. "Whales," I say stupidly.

Thomas nods. "Whales are awesome." He pauses, his eyes flicking from my eyes, to my mouth, back up to my eyes. "And so are you."

My heart downright stops. As does time, I think. The noise of the people around us is nothing but static as my world narrows down to the two of us. Thomas's blue eyes and soft lips.

Which are definitely getting closer.

"There you are!" Simon. "Why do you keep taking off with this guy without telling me?"

TWENTY-ONE

Fifteen-Year-Old Save

Thomas

I TAKE BACK anything positive I have ever thought or said about Isabelle's brother. I don't care if he's the reason I was able to "bump into" Isabelle here today. Can't he see we're busy?

"If you're just going to stand here and stare into each other's eyes, there are better places," Simon says with a huge smile as he comes to stand next to his sister. "Places that are private, calm, romantic. You know, without the slobbering kids and the murderous polar bear."

Well, Isabelle doesn't look like a vampire anymore. She is blushing furiously and her mouth is working but no sound is coming out. I *think* she's more angry than embarrassed, which is a good sign for me. Right?

Vincent, his brown hair sticking out in all directions now he's removed his beanie, comes up next to Simon. At least he has the decency to look sorry, realizing what was just interrupted.

Only when my hand starts cramping in pain do I realize I'm still holding Isabelle's hand. Her face isn't quite clear on what emotions she's feeling, but her hand is telling me it's nothing good.

So, of course, I say the first thing that comes to mind, to distract her. "Maybe a murderous polar bear is exactly right for this situation. I'll have you know they're awesome."

Simon, whose eyes haven't left his sister's since he showed up here, turns to frown at me. "Murderous polar bears are awesome?"

"Yes." I meet his gaze head on. Honestly, if he doesn't give his sister a break, I just might *become* murderous. Simon is a lot bigger than the slaughtered seal under the polar bear's paw, but I'm willing to give it a shot. Does he not see how much she hates this?

Vincent shifts from foot to foot, his usual stupid jokes conspicuously absent. I'll have to thank him later for actually having some tact for once.

Simon turns back to his sister, his expression that of someone about to make another bad joke—but when their eyes lock, he stops in his tracks. I don't know them well enough to understand the silent conversation they have, but Isabelle must have made some decent points.

"Right," Simon says. "Murderous polar bears are awesome. And so are volcanoes. Vincent, how about we go check out the different types of lava?"

If I know my friend, he has no interest whatsoever in learning about volcanoes. "Sounds great. Lead the way. Thomas, we'll talk later? Call me when you're home or something?"

I agree with a nod. Normally, I'd have shaken his hand, but Isabelle still has mine in a death grip and I have no wish to get out of it. Vincent sees our interlocked hands and gives me a pat on the shoulder before dragging Simon away.

"Your brother is…" I search for the right word. Well, the right word is cock-blocker, but I don't want to say that out loud, especially with so many kids roaming around.

Isabelle sighs. "He thinks he's helping. And going through some stuff of his own, so I don't want to be too hard on him."

We leave the polar bear behind and stroll through the rest of the exhibit without really looking at any of the animals. Our sweaty palms are plastered together and I'm overly aware of Isabelle's presence at my side. The rosy scent of her hair is haunting me whenever she steps closer to get around someone else, making me lose my train of thought. I feel like I'm sixteen again.

Except I never held a girl's hand at sixteen, of course.

"It must be weird living at home again," I say.

"*So* weird," Isabelle almost groans. "I feel like I'm in a computer game or something. I tried one option, that didn't work out, and now I'm back to a fifteen-year-old save, starting over. Except I'm not eighteen anymore so nothing seems to fit."

I chuckle. "I'm so disappointed right now. I always dreamed of being able to live my life like it was a game. Find a fortuitous spot, make a save, and try going down several different paths to see which one ends up best. And now you're telling me it isn't satisfying?"

"I guess it might be if you really did go back in time to start over. But you can't go back and keep the memories and life experiences of fifteen years and just expect to live your life like you would have at eighteen. And don't even get me *started* on the fact that the body is nowhere near the same."

Yeah, I'm not going to touch that one with a ten-foot pole. I understand what she's saying, and I guess it might even be possible that she was drop-dead gorgeous at eighteen, but I have no wish for her to be that young. Her body is absolutely perfect as it is—I don't need to see more of her than I have already to know that—and eighteen-year-olds really don't do it for me anymore. That's *way* into creepy land.

The first part of what she says shouldn't be quite as touchy, though. "But what if you could? Go back and lose the memories of the last fifteen years? Would you do it?"

We're back at the wall of skeletons but neither of us really looks at it this time as we stroll past. A couple of rays of sunlight stream through the constant layer of clouds outside and light up what I assume to be the skeleton of a dolphin. It's impressive how it looks like it's really swimming through water.

"Huh," Isabelle says. "I don't know. Just *dropping* a big chunk of my life like that because I didn't like it?" She's frowning, apparently thinking very seriously about my question. "What's to say I wouldn't make the same mistakes the second time, since I don't remember my first go at it?"

"Good point. But that means you were confident in your decision back then. That there was no other alternative you thought about choosing, or you might have chosen if one little thing had been different?"

We're close to the turnstiles and the souvenir shop at the exit. I'm letting Isabelle lead and will follow as long as she'll let me. We're apparently done with the Museum.

"This conversation got deep fast," Isabelle comments as she goes through the turnstiles first. Still not letting go of my hand, so we both end up leaning over the turnstile until it unlocks and I can follow. We both look at our interlocked hands—difficult to pretend we weren't really aware of doing it now—and I'm pretty sure I'm blushing.

"I don't know." Isabelle keeps pondering my question. "This feels like when you ask parents who haven't slept through the night in ten years if they wish they never had children. They *do*, but they don't wish their children never to have been born."

"So what you're saying is that you regret the decisions you made back then, but you don't really regret them?"

We pass through the souvenir shop and out into the cold. No choice now, we have to let go of each other's hands to put our winter coats on. Isabelle takes her beret out of a coat pocket and pulls it down to her ears, and I do the same with my beanie.

Once we're properly covered up, my heart beating furiously because I'm suddenly nervous, I grab Isabelle's hand again. Thrilled doesn't even begin to describe how I feel when her fingers curl around mine in response.

"What about you?" Isabelle asks me. "If you could go back to some 'saved' moment in your life and change something to make your life different, would you do it?"

I open my mouth to reply that of course I wouldn't. But no sound comes out.

As I stand there in front of the Museum of Natural History, surrounded by people waiting in line to get in or with their hands full of souvenirs on their way home, and the beautiful garden of the Jardin des Plantes behind me, my mind takes me on a fast rewind through my past.

Although I'm not *thrilled* with my current job, I wouldn't want to be somewhere else. I'm doing something I love and with people I respect. My two previous jobs were where I got my work experience, which allowed me to land my current job, so no regrets there, either. The five years of studying to become an engineer were the best years of my life, where I finally had friends and could do whatever I wanted without anyone ever judging me.

Which brings me to high school.

Not the best years of my life, by a long shot.

I didn't know how to be cool, or even how to pretend. The cool kids in my school considered me weird and let me know it. I mostly hung out with Vincent and a couple of other outcasts. We stuck together so we wouldn't have to be alone during recess, but calling the two other guys friends would be something of an exaggeration. Right now I can't even remember their names.

"If I could get a second go at my high school years, I would take it," I say.

"Even if it means giving up everything that happened after?"

I shrug. "The rest of it, I'd do the same. Just get rid of those three years, figure out a way to do them differently. Then back on track."

Isabelle leads the way through the Jardin des Plantes. I assume she's heading for her parents' home in the Busca neighborhood. "But how would you fix what your problem was back then without the knowledge you have now? How will fifteen-year-old Thomas know not to make the mistakes a second time?"

"Maybe I'd have better survival instincts the second time around?"

"Survival instincts?" The look Isabelle sends me is piercing. This conversation turned serious, and fast. "What exactly is it that you wish you'd done differently?"

"Honestly, if I'm wishing for the impossible, I'd rather wish for the *other* guys to change." I never talk to anyone about my high school days, but now I figure why not. What is it going to hurt that Isabelle knows I was bullied in high school? It might even help her, in a you're-not-alone kind of way. "I have a very unoriginal history of bullying."

"I see." And although there is worry in her eyes, I don't get the feeling it's because the bullying might have hurt me. Her next words confirm it. "But how can you be sure you'd have ended up on the same path if the bullies had treated you differently?

Maybe, by being included in the cool kids' group, you wouldn't have learned as much in school because you'd have been too busy partying. So you wouldn't have gotten accepted to the college you went to and might have been working the cash register of the local Aldi right now. Or—" she raises an elegant eyebrow "—you wouldn't have wanted to get away from Biarritz and you'd have studied something completely different, something you could do in your home town."

We've reached the other end of the path crossing the Jardin des Plantes and step out from yet another brick arch and onto one of the avenues leading toward Isabelle's home. The screaming kids are behind us, the growling cars ahead of us.

How did we get into such a serious discussion? And why can't I stop considering Isabelle's questions like my life depends on it? It's like I'm actually going to be sent back in time and want to make sure that this time, I'll do everything right.

"I don't think I'd have been that different if the bullies had left me alone," I say. "I didn't want to be part of their group. I just wanted to be left alone. And I think my interest in computers was strong enough that I'd have ended up in the same college here in Toulouse, even if I wasn't also running away from Biarritz."

"You *think*. You don't *know*." Isabelle's voice is distant and her eyes are on the tops of the trees lining the avenue. I get the feeling she's not really talking about me, accusing me of not knowing myself.

"Are you saying you *wouldn't* go back and change anything if you could?"

She doesn't answer straight away and we walk in silence as I let her consider her answer. We're on her parents' street, only two houses down the road, when she answers.

"I don't think I would."

TWENTY-TWO

Maybe I Did Travel Back in Time

Isabelle

How odd.

I've spent the past three weeks lamenting over my fate, feeling guilty for letting Pierre ruin my life, feeling like a failure in front of my parents, like a complete waste of space for being back to square one. And yet, when I seriously consider the possibility of going back and changing something from when I was eighteen, I don't want to do it.

What would I change?

I guess if I'd wanted to study something other than tourism and art, maybe I wouldn't have been so keen on following Pierre to England. But I *did* want to study those subjects. And I could have done that in Toulouse or pretty much any other big French city, so that's hardly a defining moment.

Wanting distance from my parents was also a deciding factor, of course. I don't think I was consciously aware of my need to get away, but in hindsight, I can see it as a major driver. I was slowly suffocating under my parents' roof and scrutiny, and it would have been very difficult to properly figure out who I was while they were watching so closely.

The thing is, it's not my entire life that's a mess right now. It's just the part involving Pierre. The rest of it—my education, my job, my friends—is exactly like I wanted it, and I wouldn't change a thing.

So I guess if I could go back and remove Pierre from the equation but keep everything else, maybe I'd do it. But chances are I *wouldn't* have ended up in the same places if I hadn't followed him when he wanted to study in England.

And my life isn't *that* bad.

I'm just going through a rough patch.

We've reached my parents' house. Even though it's early afternoon, the kitchen light is on, which probably means Maman is cooking. She claims not to need glasses but can't read the recipes without a floodlight directed at her cooking book. I hope it's cookies. With salted butter. I can't even remember the last time I had some.

I don't open the front gate but come to a stop on the sidewalk. From the look on Thomas's face, he's just fine with not coming face to face with my mother anytime soon.

"Thank you for that oddly profound conversation," I say with a smile. "It actually makes me feel a little better. Like I do have some control over my life, so maybe one day soon I'll be ready to move out of my parents' house—for the second and hopefully final time."

"Well, at least that makes one of us." Thomas doesn't quite meet my eyes and when I move to step into his line of sight, his gaze drops to our joined hands. "I guess you're a better person than me. I'd still like to have those high school years back."

"I'm sure they helped making you into who you are today. And I, for one, quite like the result."

Why am I flirting with him? Didn't I decide *not* to start anything so soon after leaving Pierre? But there's no point in trying to answer those questions. All I want is for the residual pain and insecurity I see in his eyes when he talks about high school to go away.

Nobody likes embarrassment or pain—but they're part of shaping who we are. People who have never met any kind of resistance are usually uninteresting and lacking in empathy.

Thomas, who forgave me for hitting him—twice!—without a second thought, clearly has his fair share of empathy. And it's such a fresh change from Pierre, I *need* to keep seeing him. Bring my faith in humanity back up.

Thomas's gaze slowly works its way up to lock onto mine. We're close enough that I can make out the two spots of yellow in each of his sparkling blue eyes, and a fingerprint on the outside edge of his glasses.

Neither of us says anything. Time slows down, the noise of the cars driving past taking a back seat to the heartbeat in my chest and my entire being feeling so much lighter than I can ever remember. Slowly, we close the gap—I can't tell if it's him or me, probably a little bit of both—until our noses touch.

With his breath mixing with mine, my lips stretch into a huge smile. And I lean in that last inch to kiss him.

I think I might have taken him by surprise. He draws in a sharp breath. Then he quickly catches on to what's happening, and seals his lips over mine while pulling our joined hands up between our chests and his free arm around my waist to pull me closer.

That thing about melting into a kiss? I totally understand it now. My free hand on Thomas's chest, I lean into him even more, plastering myself to his front and pushing onto my toes to get closer to his height. My smile is long gone, replaced by molding my lips to his, enjoying the soft brush of his stubble on my face and his breath on my cheek.

I feel like I'm eighteen again and getting my first kiss.

Maybe I *did* travel back in time.

I twitch slightly as a car door slams close behind me. Right, we're not exactly in private, but on the sidewalk of a relatively busy street in the middle of the afternoon. Still, prolonging the kiss just a *little* longer surely can't hurt—

"Isabelle! What the hell do you think you're doing?" The familiar voice turns my blood to ice and I freeze in place. My breathing stops.

Pierre.

I try to scramble away from Thomas, "try" being the operative word. My body doesn't seem to work properly and I step away while still on my tiptoes and my lips puckered. I can't stop blinking, as if my brain is trying to reboot over and over, without success. When I realize my hand is still on Thomas's chest, I snatch it away as if I'm burnt—which is when I start to topple backward.

"Whoa, careful there." Although Thomas also twitched when Pierre started yelling, his reaction was nowhere near as violent as mine. He's still holding onto my hand even though my grip has gone slack, and he pulls me back into a proper vertical position with the arm that's around my waist.

On the street, no more than ten meters away, a taxi has stopped with its emergency lights on. Pierre is already halfway to join us when the passenger window lowers and a woman's voice calls out. "I told you I can't stay here, Monsieur! Get your things out of the trunk or I'm taking them with me."

Pierre's growl and eye-roll has ice running down my spine. When he turns to direct his anger at the taxi driver, I'm flooded with relief—and shame.

How could I have let him have such power over me?

"Your ex-husband, I presume?" Thomas says, his voice low. Pierre is getting his bags from the trunk, loudly, so the risk of him overhearing are slim to none, but I appreciate Thomas making the effort.

My reply is barely audible. "Yes."

Thomas sighs. "Excellent." He gives my hand a squeeze.

God, we're still holding hands. And Pierre is *right there*, stomping toward us with his fancy gray carry-on that he was so proud of getting as a gift from his boss a couple of years back. His eyes might as well be shooting arrows and his jaw is working so furiously, I worry for the state of his teeth.

Why is he here?

"Really, Isabelle?" he thunders as he drops his precious suitcase on the sidewalk. "Really? You leave without a word, refuse to take any of my calls, and when I come to see you, you're *sucking face* with *some guy*?"

The fact that everything he just said is perfectly true somehow calms me down. Seems like I expected him to make up some outlandish tales, put words in my mouth, and make me feel guilty for leaving him.

How weird is it that I'm surprised to hear the truth coming out of my husband's mouth?

"That sounds about right," I say. "I didn't take you for someone who couldn't take a hint, Pierre."

A truck roars past, but I don't think anyone would have said anything even in perfect silence. Pierre's expression is comically close to the cartoon version of surprised, and I think Thomas just choked on nothing.

Pierre snaps back in action. "A *hint*? You call walking out on our life a *hint*? What happened to improving our communication skills? And working on our marriage? Not giving up at the first obstacle?" He's in my face, screaming so loud the owner of the liquor store across the street comes out to see what's going on. A drop of spit lands on my cheek.

There's the husband I remember. Most of the time I felt like he didn't hear a word I said. My words went in one ear and straight out the other.

But when he needed ammo to make me feel guilty? Out came the proof that he'd heard every single word.

I don't rise to the bait this time, though. The reason I never took his calls is that I was afraid he'd manage to get his claws in me again. That I'd feel guilty and go crawling back.

Seems like I needn't have worried. I can see his manipulation for what it is now—and I don't care anymore. Not about our life together, certainly not about our marriage.

Thomas, however, isn't used to Pierre's temper tantrums. He puts his free hand on Pierre's chest. "Would you mind stepping back a step, Monsieur?"

My entire body tenses in sync with Pierre's. Politeness never worked well with him. I think it makes him conscious of the fact that he's *not* being polite, and he doesn't like it.

Pierre steps into Thomas's personal space, so close their noses are close to touching. "How's this, *Monsieur*? Is that better? Do you have any other requests for when I talk to *my wife*?"

This isn't going to end well. I search for something to say that will calm Pierre down without letting him have his way, but the problem was always that there *is* no other way to calm him down.

"I really think it would be a good idea if you—"

That's as far as Thomas gets before Pierre takes a step back—and throws a punch at Thomas's face.

TWENTY-THREE

I Should Learn to Duck

Thomas

HERE WE GO again.

The world moves in slow motion and I watch my third shiner in as many weeks come toward me. Not slow enough for me to stop it, unfortunately. I should learn to duck.

His half-closed fist hits me in the jaw. My head snaps sideways. Pain flares through my face as I stumble two steps backward.

It doesn't hurt as much as when Isabelle punched me.

I realize I'm no longer holding her hand. Did she let go or did I? As I blink to get the world to focus, I see her pushing at her ex-husband, screaming at him in anger.

I can barely focus on Isabelle who is less than two meters away from me. The other side of the street is a gray blur with vertical lines of brown. My glasses. I search the ground around me. There.

Damn it. They're broken. *Again*.

I whirl to face the man, annoyed that I won't be able to see him properly. I can tell that he's a good head taller than Isabelle, probably about her age with a trendy beard and slicked-back dark hair, and a designer leather jacket that probably cost what I make in a month.

"You owe me four hundred euros," I tell the jerk. "You broke my glasses."

He gives me a once-over before looking away, as if deciding I'm not even worthy of an answer. To Isabelle, he sneers, "Will you stop being so hysterical? You're making a scene."

Oh God, he's *such* a sleaze-ball. I *hate* guys like him. This is what my high school bullies will have grown into. This is where they end up. Still treating other people like crap, walking all over them and spreading misery.

And the thing I hate the most? That my first reflex is *still* to cringe and run away.

Isabelle doesn't stop yelling, though. If this tactic of his worked on her when they were married, it has lost its effectiveness. "I'm not hysterical, Pierre. I'm angry! Pissed off that you just waltz in here and *hit* a man for no good reason!"

"You're *my wife*! That's reason en—"

"I'm not done talking!" She pushes him in the chest, forcing him to take a step back. "You know why I haven't taken any of your calls, Pierre? It's because I don't want to listen to you anymore. You've manipulated me for years, made me feel worthless for years, and *I'm done*! You hear me? *Done!*"

I'm fairly certain I'm mirroring the ex's stunned expression. Except mine is based in awe, and his in shock. Guess he never knew she was a fighter.

My hand goes to my jaw. It's painful and sore, but nowhere near as bad as either of the times Isabelle hurt me.

I can't help it, I let out a laugh at the thought.

The ex, who doesn't seem to know what to do with Isabelle's anger, tears free of her hold and advances on me, threatening finger pointed right at my face. "What's so funny? Do I need to repeat myself?" Then he winces and opens and closes his hands like it's hurting him.

"Are you threatening to hit me *again*?" My body's not happy with me staying put—heart beating furiously, stomach twisting, palms sweating—but if there's one thing I've learned, it's that you never let the bullies win. You let them get the upper hand and prove that their tactics are working once, and you're doomed.

"I wouldn't recommend it," I tell him, staring him straight in the eyes. "Hitting me once in anger isn't going to look good when I tell the police about it, but *twice*? That second one is quite obviously premeditated." I touch my jaw again, pretending to assess the damage. "Your ex-wife throws a better punch than you, by the way. I'm not even sure what that was. A slap or a punch? Or something in-between? Is that why your hand's hurting? You didn't even know to make a proper fist before making contact?"

I say that as if I would never run the risk of hitting someone so unprofessionally, when I've never hit anyone in my life. I have, however, read extensively, and I know throwing a punch can hurt as much as receiving it sometimes.

And the jerk doesn't know if I'm a pure geek or a karate expert. Let him wonder.

The tick in his jaw gives me the answer to my question. Serves him right if he broke something.

"Now, about the glasses," I say and hold them up so he can see the damage he did. This time, both lenses are broken, though the frames seem intact. "These are brand new. You owe me four hundred euros." He doesn't need to know that's the total cost and replacing the lenses will only cost about half.

The jerk sneers. "I'm not going to give you four hundred euros for a pair of lousy hipster glasses. You don't even need to pay for glasses in France."

"You're not only ignorant on the art of punching someone in the face, but also on the subject of medical costs in France?" I'm getting into my stride here, bringing up long-dormant skills of getting back at the bullies the only way I could—by using my brain. I'm staying alert, though, because I believe he's capable of delivering on his promise of a second attack. He might not hit as well as Isabelle, but that's no reason to run unnecessary risks.

"I can only get 'free' glasses every two years. If they break before that time is up, I have to pay for them. So this means *you'll* have to pay for them. Since you broke them." I look him up and down. "You look like the kind of guy who would carry that kind of sum in cash."

"I'm not giving you money!"

"Right. I'll just call the police and have them clear this up." I take out my phone. *Should* I call the police? I'm not sure if a slap/punch in the face is enough to justify bringing them here.

"No need to call the police." I whip around, and come face to face with Isabelle's mother. In a dark blue pants suit instead of pajamas this time, and her dark hair in a loose bun at the nape of her neck. She has one foot on the sidewalk as she holds the iron gate to her property open. Her expression is so neutral it's almost scary.

"Vivienne," the jerk says, his voice suddenly honeyed. "I'm so happy to see you. You wouldn't believe the sight that greeted me when I arrived just now."

I hold my breath. I'm the outsider here, the one who doesn't know any of the others well enough to anticipate how they'll react.

Isabelle has turned vampire-white again. Even from where I'm standing, I can see her shortness of breath and widened eyes. Her hands are twitching, like they did when she was stressing out in the airplane lavatory when we first met. Eyes skipping from her ex-husband to her mother and back again, I don't think she knows where this situation will go either.

The jerk seems confident he'll get the mother on his side, which I don't like. If the two of them team up on Isabelle, I might have to steal her away. I'm not leaving her here to let them double-tag her.

The mother should be playing poker. I have *no* idea what she thinks of the situation, though I know she has recognized me, noticed the broken glasses and the jerk's suitcase. Probably even the clenching hopefully-broken fist.

The jerk seems to take her silence as an invitation to elaborate.

"I take time off from work to come here because my wife has upped and left me without as much as a note, and she refuses to take my calls. I get out of the taxi after a long day of traveling, and there she is, *kissing* some stranger."

I have to give it to him, he's a pretty good actor. If I hadn't known the backstory, I would have taken him for a devoted husband who just got stabbed in the back.

What worries me is the look of fear on Isabelle's face. And it's not directed at her ex.

She doesn't expect her mother to have her back.

I inch closer to her and put a hand at the small of her back, showing her I'm here for her. I also map out the quickest route to the metro, ready to literally run away with Isabelle and take her to my place if needed.

The mother's gaze doesn't stray from Pierre's. "I see you're behaving like a good husband who is worried for the well-being of his wife."

Oh God, she's really going to take the jerk's side?

The man seems to inflate when he realizes his plan is working. "I am worried about her. She—"

"That would certainly be a first." There's no change in tone, or inflection. Very polite, as if discussing the weather over a cup of coffee. "Twelve years of marriage and you've never done a single thing for the well-being of my daughter. You've only ever done things that were in your own best interest. Why would you change now?"

TWENTY-FOUR

Pierre Owes Him Four Hundred Euros

Isabelle

THERE'S NO WAY I heard that right.

I'm vaguely aware of Thomas's hand on my back but my entire focus is on the woman staring down my ex-husband from her front step. What are the chances of aliens having descended and taken over my mother's body? Somehow, that feels more likely than her standing up for me.

That *is* what she said, right? That Pierre was never a good husband?

Pierre seems to be as shell-shocked as me. His mouth is moving but no sound comes out. His eyes go to me—and he finds his voice. "I've always had your best interest at heart. Always. I'm only ever trying to help."

I don't know what to do with Maman defending me, but I'm quite familiar with Pierre trying to manipulate me. And I'm not having any more of it. Stepping closer, I give him my most angry stare. "You never tried to *help* me. You tried to fix me. Get me to behave in the way you wanted. Be the wife you needed to get ahead in life. And always with the smarmy tone and the stupid arguments that I needed to sacrifice yet another thing I loved for *us*. Well, that's bullshit!"

I think I hear Thomas whistle softly behind me.

Pierre and I are both about to say something, but Maman interrupts us. "Why don't we take this inside?"

I know that tone. She doesn't want us airing our dirty laundry on the sidewalk. For once, considering the number of people who have stopped to stare, I agree. I'm able to admit to myself that I've let Pierre manipulate me for too long, but that doesn't mean I want everybody and their grandmother to know.

"As long as he's not staying," I say. "And Thomas is coming, too. Pierre owes him four hundred euros." I grab Thomas's hand and pull him along past my still-expressionless mother, through the gate, and up the four steps to the front door.

Thomas stumbles on the last step and he mumbles something about being half-blind without his glasses.

Inside, before the others come through the door, I gently press my hand to his jaw. "Did he hurt you? Would you like that bag of frozen peas you didn't get the last time?"

He smiles and his kind eyes find mine. "I'm fine. I was serious about you being much better at packing a punch. This should hardly bruise at all."

I'm tempted to kiss him again, but then Pierre storms through the door, dumping his suitcase by the kitchen counter, and Maman glides in behind him, gently shutting the door.

Pierre doesn't waste any time. "I can't believe you made me come all this way just to talk to you, Isabelle. How hard can it be to pick up the phone when your husband calls?"

"I didn't have anything to say to you," I say.

"Well, I had something to say to you!" Splotches of red appear on Pierre's cheeks and the tendons in his neck are standing out. It's very similar to how he looked that last night, when he threatened to hit me.

"I heard you loud and clear when you told me you would hurt me if I didn't do what you wanted. Figured I wouldn't hang around to see if you were bluffing."

Breathing heavily, Pierre's angry stare leaves my face for a moment. Checking the reactions of the two other people in the room.

"Worried what they'll think, Pierre? You should be. They're seeing you in all your manipulative and abusive glory for the first time."

"Oh, I didn't need for him to be this explicit to know what kind of man he was." Maman's poker face is still on, but a hint of scorn has entered her voice. "Why do you think I was always so frustrated with your decision to stay with him?"

That brings me up short. She knew Pierre was abusive? "Why didn't you say anything?"

"I did." Although she's talking to me, her eyes are on Pierre. Assessing the threat. "But you can't convince someone in an abusive relationship to get out just by saying they're being manipulated. They have to come to that conclusion themselves. You would simply have come home and called even more rarely than you already did, *chérie*."

So she convinced me she would never respect any decision I ever made on my own instead. I knew she didn't like Pierre but I honestly thought it was because I picked him and by default, I never made any good choices.

Pierre *wasn't* a good choice, of course, but he was hardly the only decision my mother had opinions about.

I'll have to hash this out with her later, though. I'm not getting into a conversation with such high probability of me breaking down while Pierre and Thomas are both in the room.

Pierre has calmed himself down. I can practically see the mask falling into place. "Isabelle, I need you to come home with me right now. Get your things and I'll call a taxi so we can get on the first flight back to England."

"No, Pierre. Me wanting a separation wasn't a rash decision I'll go back on. You're going back home alone." My senses seem to be hyper-aware all of a sudden. I can hear the air vent in the kitchen opening and closing, and the familiar smell of old coffee from the pot in the corner where Papa always likes to leave half a cup, "just in case." I'm mapping out the quickest route out of the house.

If Pierre is ever going to carry through on his promise to hit me, this is when it'll happen.

Thomas steps in front of me, putting himself between me and Pierre.

He has made the same assessment of Pierre's state of mind and is defending me. That's so sweet and brave, but I can't let him get hurt because of me *again*. He's become a human punching ball since we met on that plane.

I pull on his elbow until he comes to stand between me and Maman. "I won't let you get hurt again because of me."

Maman speaks up, this time in the tone of voice that usually meant I'd be grounded for a month. "This is where you turn tail and run, Pierre. Pay the man what you owe for his glasses, take your fancy suitcase, and go back to England. Without your *ex*-wife."

Pierre turns his angry glare on Maman.

"Give me what you owe and leave," Thomas says. "Or I'll go to the police to press charges."

At this point, I'll be happy as long as he leaves. I'll pay for the repair of Thomas's glasses myself. I'm pretty sure I owe him for the last time, anyway.

But it seems Pierre has finally realized he's fighting a losing battle. Fuming so hard I'm surprised there isn't steam coming out of his ears, he forcefully opens his jacket, gets his wallet from the inner pocket, and tears out six fifty-euro bills. Because yes, he is the type of guy who likes having a lot of cash on hand.

He throws the bills toward Thomas and while they billow down to the hardwood floor, grabs his suitcase and marches out the front door, slamming it shut behind him.

The three of us stand there in the reverberating silence, staring at the door.

I have no idea what to say. What is there to say when you've just had an extremely embarrassing fight with your ex in front of your judgmental mother and the guy you're currently crushing on?

I wish I could pretend it never happened.

That won't work, of course.

Should I pick up the money? Turn tail and leave the room, letting Thomas fend for himself with my mother? Question my mother on why she kept her opinion of Pierre to herself for all these years?

I'm still undecided when the front door reopens. I twitch, worried Pierre has decided he won't give up so easily.

Thankfully it's Simon. Followed by Vincent with his red pom-pom beanie.

"I could have sworn I just saw Pierre in a taxi," Simon begins, his face animated as if he wants us in on his joke. When he takes in our faces, his laughing expression falls. "It was him? What was he doing here? What did he do? Why didn't you call me?" He rushes to me, holds my hands in his. "Are you okay?"

I take a deep breath, hoping my voice will hold. "I'm fine. He's going back to England."

"Why are there a bunch of fifty-euro bills on the floor?"

"That's for my glasses." Thomas holds up his ruined glasses in explanation.

The frown on Simon's forehead deepens and he's squeezing my hands a little too hard. "He hit *you*? Why?"

"Because he was with me." I give my brother's hands a hard squeeze. He'd better know to let that go.

Simon looks from Thomas to me and back again, clearly putting two and two together. But he doesn't say anything. Instead, he leans in to look closer at Thomas's face. "Do you need something cold? Doesn't look so bad this time."

Thomas grins, flashing his crooked tooth. "Your sister throws a much better punch than her ex-husband."

Simon roars with laughter, so loudly it makes the rest of us jump. Stepping between us, Simon throws one arm over my shoulder and one over Thomas's. "I like this guy, Isa. I'm telling you, you should keep him."

TWENTY-FIVE

Pet Monkeys and American Spies

Thomas

"You went ice skating and fell on your face."

"You have a pet monkey who decided he'd had enough of your bullshit and hit you."

"You're a spy working for the Americans and someone almost blew your cover."

I turn to stare at Benjamin. "Americans?"

Lifting his hands from his keyboard as if I'm pointing a gun at him, Benjamin widens his eyes. "The Russians are hardly interested in our apps, boss. The Americans are the real competition."

I huff. "Clément is talking about pet monkeys and you're worried about whether I'm a Russian spy or an American one?"

How did I end up here?

Oh, right. By deciding not to tell my colleagues about the origins of my shiners. I guess one would have blown over relatively quick. Two would have kept them going for every lunch break until summer, at the very least. Three? The spy story probably makes sense.

"Somebody's using you as a punching ball," Benjamin says. "I just want to know if we should be worried. Either that you'll get hit a fourth time and be out of commission for months, leaving us in the lurch, or that whoever is after you will show up here, and we'll all end up black and blue."

I run a hand down my face, pinching my nose under my out-of-fashion backup glasses. "You have nothing to worry about, Ben. Nobody's going to show up here to hit any of us."

Clément snaps his fingers and winks at me. "Because he's decided he's had enough of the violent monkey and sold it back to the circus he stole it from."

Benjamin and I both stare at Clément slack-jawed.

"Thomas, I have questions." Anita leans over my desk, a notebook in hand. I didn't see her get up from her seat, much less approach. Maybe she's the Russian spy.

I think I manage to keep the flinch off my face. "Yes?"

"About these categories. How many are there? Do I just use the three you mentioned in the ticket? I did a quick search online and I think there might be some more. And I'm not sure how to automatically detect which category each location goes in." With her unnerving stare fixed on me, she clicks her pen open and stands ready to write in her notebook any answer I might have for her.

Except I don't have one, of course. I don't know anything about museums. I just copy/pasted the comment from Isabelle's review into the ticket and hoped Anita would know what to do with it.

I've known Anita long enough to know when she comes to me with her notepad ready, I better have answers. She's not going back to her desk without them.

The way I see it, I have two options: open Google while she's staring at me and read off my search results, thereby losing all credibility in her eyes, or go straight to my source.

I've been toying with asking Simon for his sister's number since Sunday. The guy quite clearly likes me, he damn well gave his blessing in their parents' living room. I'm pretty sure he'd give me his sister's number—or at the very least give my number to his sister—and probably wouldn't give me *too* much of a hard time over it.

But I'm worried what Isabelle might think. She's been quite clear on not wanting to start up anything new right now, so soon after leaving her husband. When we accidentally meet, or "accidentally" meet, there's less pressure. We just happen to be in the same place with no agenda or expectations, and we're allowed to have fun. If I ask her out on a date, I know it's going to be too much too soon for her.

Now, where on that scale would I place needing help with developing my app?

Screw it, I'm going to try it. If for nothing else, to get Anita back to her desk and her uncanny eyes off me.

Thomas: *Hi Simon, your sister left a very helpful review on one of my apps. I need more details. Would you mind passing her my number and ask if she'd mind having a little chat with my colleague?*

The reply is almost immediate.

Simon: *Your flirting game is weird, dude.*

Simon: *Isa tells me if I don't write something nice she'll tell Maman I'm home because I got a girl pregnant. Since I don't want to be a father just yet: awesome excuse to talk to my* *sister, dude. You rock. I'm giving her your number before she has me married with two children. I'm out.*

I can't help but laugh. This guy is ridiculous. And clearly a very good brother, something I'm happy Isabelle has. Her ex-husband is a jerk and from what I've gathered, her parents weren't the best. We all need *someone* in our corner.

I glance up at Anita. Pen still poised over her notebook. Dark eyes still on me. She's completely expressionless, yet I'm pretty sure she's judging me.

I jump as my phone buzzes with a message. The corner of Anita's lips twitch. I decide to ignore her and unlock my phone instead.

Unknown: *Hi, Isabelle here. Simon says you needed something for the app?*

I save her number to my phone, butterflies in my stomach and a stupid grin on my face.

Thomas: *Hi! Thank you for replying. I showed your review to one of my developers and she has questions. You wouldn't happen to be available for a quick consultation?*

I hit send then sit staring at my phone, holding my breath. Was that too impersonal? Too direct? Should I have chatted a bit first? Asked her out for a drink to mention Anita when we're face to face?

Isabelle: *That sounds like a great distraction from the French administration. What's the best way of communicating with the developer? Email? Text? Phone?*

I barely have time to open my mouth to ask Anita what she prefers when the next message comes through.

Isabelle: *In person?*

My breath catches in my throat. Isabelle would come here?

It's possible. Our offices are right next to a metro station, on the same line that stops less than five hundred meters from where Isabelle lives. She wouldn't offer if she didn't want to come, right?

"I think walking into a door is unfortunately our best bet," Benjamin says loudly to Clément. "He's been staring at his phone like a zombie for a whole minute. Who knows what happens if he does that while out in the world."

If I bring Isabelle here, will the guys learn where I got the black eyes?

Nah, I should be safe. Isabelle is a lot more embarrassed by having hit me than I am at being hit. And it's not embarrassment *per se*. I just don't want all the attention and stupid commentary.

Thomas: *If you don't mind making the trip, we'd love to have you over for a visit. You available right now?*

I send her the address. While I wait for an answer, I turn to Anita. Pen still poised. "I'll get you in touch with the person who wrote the review. She'll give you all the details you need."

Anita's eyebrows shoot up. It's the biggest reaction I've ever seen from the woman. "Are we allowed to know who the individual reviewers are and contact them?"

"No, of course not." My tone is quite brusque, but I need to be firm on this. Both to let them know *I* haven't broken any rules and to tell them *they* aren't allowed to do it. "It was written by someone I know, is all."

"Right." Anita clicks her pen closed. "And they're coming here?"

On cue, my phone buzzes.

Isabelle: *I'll be there in twenty.*

"She's coming here." My voice is breathy with stress, dammit. I try to visualize Isabelle in my office, meeting my weird colleagues, tasting our stale coffee.

I grab my coat. "I'm going out for some pastries."

TWENTY-SIX

First Contact Made and No Injuries

Isabelle

Thomas's office building is one of those gray box buildings from the seventies, the kind that makes you think of office drones and depressing sameness day in and day out. I'm on the sidewalk, my back to the allées Jean Jaurès, Toulouse's largest avenue, cutting from the train station on one end to the Capitole on the other, afternoon traffic zooming past. The weather is overcast with no hope of sun in sight and the temperature somewhere close to zero. I'm wearing a red scarf bundled around my neck in addition to my black beret and I'm really regretting not packing up more of my things before leaving England—my feet are cold.

I don't even know why I offered to come here. Answering the questions about the app won't take more than five minutes and could have been done over the phone, possibly by text.

Who am I kidding? I know why I offered to come. What I *don't* know is where I found the courage to follow through on it.

Of course, I'm only in front of the building. There's still time to turn tail and tell Thomas I'd prefer to talk to his colleague on the phone instead. That would be the sensible thing to do. What will allow me to move on with my life on my own, without a guy to lean on, to influence my decisions.

Changing my mind because I'm scared of my reaction when I meet Thomas isn't brave, though. It isn't the adult thing to do. I just need a minute to get my heartbeat under control.

A guy in a black beanie strides up to the building's front door. When he pulls it open, he glances my way, and stops. It's Thomas. Gaping at me as if he can't fathom what I'm doing here. He's carrying a brown paper bag of what I assume is pastries.

Smiling, I walk up to him. No turning back now. "Hi, Thomas. Glad to see I found the right place."

His mouth snaps shut. He glances down at the pastries in what I think is embarrassment, though I can't see what the problem would be. "Isabelle. I'm so happy you could come. Has it been twenty minutes already?"

"I may have overestimated the time it would take Simon to kick me out of the house. I, uh…" I'm in front of him now, close enough to admire the beauty of his blue eyes, to see his scruff is a little longer than the last time we met. And this is where we're supposed to do *la bise*.

We both make a slight movement toward the other, testing the waters. Right or left? I can't even remember which way Simon had us go the last time, and now that I'm close enough to see the yellow spots in his blue eyes and recognize his earthy smell, I might not be able to tell left from right.

"Left cheek?" Thomas says, his voice almost inaudible because of the cars roaring past behind me. His eyes jump down to my lips, then back up to my eyes. He's smiling, laughing at our inside joke, but the slight blush high on his cheeks tells me he's just as nervous as I am.

I'm tempted to simply go in for a kiss on the lips. Yeah, yeah, not supposed to be kissing any new guys yet. But it's *so* very tempting.

A woman rushes past us, practically pushing Thomas out of the way to get inside, and the moment is broken.

This is his workplace. Hardly the right place to start making out. So I lean way too far out on my right, making sure we don't accidentally head-butt each other, and we greet each other like the almost-strangers we are. His scruff against my cheek is soft and my hand is halfway to his face to touch it before I realize what's happening and snap my hand back in my coat pocket.

"First contact made and no injuries," Thomas says. "I say we're making progress."

"Funny. You better watch out, though. Day's not over yet."

"Good point." Thomas steps into the vestibule, holding the door for me. "Welcome to my office. You'll see, it's just as beautiful and fascinating upstairs as it is down here."

The vestibule matches the outside. Various shades of gray, all straight angles, reminiscent of a prison. Two elevators greet us straight ahead, but Thomas leads me to the stairs on the right.

"I hope you don't mind taking the stairs. It's only two floors. The elevators break down at least once a week. There's no risk of dying or anything, but getting stuck in there for an hour isn't a fun experience. Especially if you're stuck with Anita." That last part is mumbled and I don't think he said it for my benefit.

"The stairs are fine." I follow him through the door. The staircase is even more depressing and claustrophobic than the vestibule, complete with coffee stains on the walls and burn marks on a couple of the puke-green steps.

"I'm having some serious second thoughts about inviting you here," Thomas says on a sigh. "You know how you look at your own home from an outside point of view when you have someone come to visit for the first time? And suddenly you see all the ugly and weird stuff you've learned to filter out?"

"Don't worry about how the staircase in your office building looks, Thomas," I say as we pass the first floor. This place doesn't even have any windows and the only light is coming from shifty neon lighting that's probably been there since the seventies. It's like we've traveled back in time.

I sigh. "When you came to the place I'm currently calling home, you were punched by my ex-husband and witnessed our latest fight. I wouldn't worry too much about first impressions. I've got you covered."

"Hmmm." We've reached the second floor and Thomas holds the door for me, his kind eyes on mine. "That wasn't the first time I saw your home, though. The first time I went through the door head first, getting blood all over your mother's pajamas. I didn't really look at the house all that much, to be honest."

I give him a flat stare. "Thank you for reminding me. That's exactly what I needed before meeting a bunch of new people."

He smiles and puts a hand at the small of my back, making my heart do a back-flip. "You have nothing to worry about, Isabelle." He leans in as if he's about to tell me a secret. "They're a bunch of geeks. My greatest worry is that none of them will get anything done while you're here, especially with this whole sexy French girl look you've got going today."

His compliment floods me with pleasure. He thinks I'm sexy?

After a glance at what I assume to be the door to his office—from the dark and depressing hallway we've emerged into—Thomas winces. "By the way... Would it be too much to ask to not mention the fact that you're the one who gave me the black eyes? I've, uh...not managed that situation perfectly."

I look up into his eyes, trying to understand what he's saying. "What does that mean, exactly?"

"I've, uh, sort of..." Averting his eyes, he takes a deep breath. "I've refused to tell them how I got hurt. And they turn out to be a lot more curious than I bargained for."

A small part of me is hurt that he's embarrassed. What, it's impossible for a woman to land a good punch? I certainly left more of a mark on Thomas than Pierre did.

Which is a really weird and stupid thought, even if it's only in my head. I'm not *proud* of having punched the poor man!

"I'm so sorry to have put you in this situation," I settle on saying. "And several times at that."

His sweet smile makes the hallway feel a lot lighter, all of a sudden. "I'm not complaining. At all." He brushes the back of his knuckles on my cheek and he's a lot closer. "Every bruise was worth it. I just don't generally share too much personal stuff with my colleagues. Don't want to give them ammunition."

He steps away and gestures toward a door with a small sign on it. "On that note, let me introduce you to my team of geeks."

TWENTY-SEVEN

I Preen Like the Rest of Them

Thomas

OUR OFFICE MIGHT be ugly, but it has decent heating. Isabelle removes her scarf and beret but not before the jaw of every guy—and Anita—drops at the sight of her. Place the woman on the Champs Elysées and you'll have the perfect sexy French woman cliché. Maybe I could offer to be the guy to recreate the famous picture of a couple kissing…

Mind back to the present, Thomas. I'm at the office. *Not* the time to be daydreaming. Or giving away my crush to my colleagues.

I introduce Isabelle to everyone on my team. When I give one detail on each guy, telling her what he's especially good at, they all preen proudly. Can't say I blame them—I like looking good in front of Isabelle too—but I'm kind of embarrassed on their behalf. Is this really all it takes to place us firmly in a pretty woman's pocket?

"You have a good team," Isabelle says when I offer for her to leave her coat at my desk. "They seem to respect you. And have a multitude of specialties."

And I preen like the rest of them.

"There's one person left." The smile I'm directing at Isabelle falls slightly when I notice the surprised expressions on Benjamin and Clément's faces. You'd think they've never seen me smile before.

Pushing that thought aside, I lead Isabelle to Anita's corner. They shake hands. "Anita's the one who's developing what you suggested in your review on the categories of museums, galleries, and all that. A quick brainstorming on what you meant and answering Anita's questions would be most helpful."

"Of course." Isabelle grabs the chair Anita has fetched for her and smiles at Anita. "I've always loved going to museums and such. You wouldn't believe how thrilled I am to be able to help."

Well, that's news to me. Not that she'd like helping, but that she's such a big fan of museums. I figured the Sunday trip to the Museum of Natural History was simply a way to pass time. From the look on Anita's face, she finds this as weird as I do.

"I never got around to ask you what you did for a living in England." I've talked about *my* job, but all I know about hers is that she had to leave it behind when she returned to France.

Excellent job on the listening, Thomas. Just excellent.

Isabelle doesn't seem to hold a grudge, though. She smiles up at me, clearly happy to share. "I worked at a travel agency. Specialized in trips to more...cultural destinations. If someone wanted a beautiful ocean and long beaches, I sent them to one of my colleagues, but if they wanted museums, art, history...I was in my element. I studied history and travel in university."

"I didn't even know that was possible," Anita mutters. Her face doesn't show any more emotion than usual, but there's curiosity in her tone.

"Lots of people study history," Isabelle says.

"She means travel." I go grab the chair of a colleague who's on vacation for the week and sit down across from Isabelle. "You can get a diploma in *travel*?"

Isabelle rolls her eyes. This must not be the first time she gets a question of the kind. "My degree is in history. But I took all the courses I could on travel. Cultural differences, archeology, diplomacy when I could get it... I've always loved traveling, and I found I enjoyed sending other people off on adventures too."

I have a million and one questions. But we're at work, my entire team is watching, and Isabelle is here to do a quick debrief with Anita. If I want to ask questions, I'll have to man up and ask Isabelle out on a real date.

Before I can blurt out the question immediately, Anita luckily takes over. "Well, that certainly explains why you've got so many ideas for the app." She turns her computer screen so Isabelle can see. "You mentioned these three categories for museums and such. But I did a quick Google search and found a couple of others that I thought it might be interesting to include."

And off they go. Isabelle inches forward with each question, using her hands to illustrate, pointing at the screen when she explains what she wants in various parts of the app, always giving justifications and real-life examples.

Anita is jotting it all down on her notebook. She's good at this. If there's something she hasn't understood, she'll have Isabelle explain it again from another angle. Whenever they finish a feature, she makes a quick summary, in her own words, to make sure she understood everything.

Love at First Flight

The girl might be a little odd, but she's brilliant at her job. This is why I tolerate her stares day in and day out.

I don't even realize I've stayed in place until Benjamin makes a comment. "I'm starting to think a girl had something to do with it. Clearly, his mind's not all present when in the company of a beautiful woman, and would be quite capable of walking into doors."

Have I stayed in my seat, watching Anita and Isabelle work for over fifteen minutes? Why, yes, I have. It's a wonder I'm not drooling.

Isabelle spares a quick frowning glance at Benjamin, but continues her explanation of the different levels of information users might want depending on their goal for the visit.

I would be in the "just wants a quick look around and the fun facts" category, in case you were wondering. Isabelle, clearly, is of the "wants to know everything about everything" variety.

Forcing myself to push away from Anita's desk, I return to my own chair while glaring daggers at Benjamin. "Will you cut it with the conspiracy theories?"

Benjamin frowns. "It's not a conspiracy theory. That would imply some outside force manipulating you to walk into doors. Ah! Okay, yeah. Pretty woman. Outside force. I guess I can see that. But why would a pretty girl like Isabelle want you to walk into doors? It all seems like too much trouble for too little result to me."

"If she wanted him to get a shiner," Clément says, "she could have just hit him herself. That would probably have been easier. Less planning."

I better not be blushing. I focus as best I can on my annoyance with my two colleagues instead of the embarrassment of them finding out the truth. I would never hear the end of it.

"Don't you two have anything better to do than badmouthing Isabelle while she's giving away her expertise for free so our apps can be better?"

Benjamin's eyebrow jumps up. "We're just shooting the shit, like usual. No need to get all bossy on us."

"I *am* your boss."

"Yes, but you don't behave like it. We do what you say because what you say makes sense, not because you're the boss man and if we don't follow orders we'll get fired. Why should that change now?"

"Can't be the presence of a woman," Clément muses, tapping his chewed-up ballpoint pen against his lower lip like he's the world's cheapest private eye. "Anita has been here for two years and he's never behaved weirdly around her."

"No, but *Anita* is weird. Maybe this is how he behaves around normal women."

"I heard that." Anita's eyes don't leave her notepad.

I barely bite back my groan. So Isabelle is also hearing everything the idiots are saying? Maybe she can come over here and punch them for me.

"You're kinda proving my point, Anita," Benjamin says, undeterred. "Seriously, though. She can't have made him walk into *three* doors, can she? I mean, she's gorgeous, but not *that* gorgeous."

I have no idea what to say to get them to shut up. I don't know how Isabelle will feel about them commenting on her looks like this. I can't agree with them because that would make things awkward with Isabelle and it would give them incentive to continue. I can't contradict them, because she *is* gorgeous and I'm not going to hurt her feelings just to protect myself in front of my colleagues.

My mind's running in circles searching for a solution, trying to figure out how to stay cool but not hurt Isabelle.

I'm seriously considering setting off the fire alarm when Anita does the job for me. "Time to shut up, guys. Or I'm going to see the big boss about sexual harassment."

All three of us stare slack-jawed across the room. Did she just—

I snap back before the other two. Anita found the solution to my problem, not to mention the fact that she's right, and I need to take advantage of this opportunity.

"You heard her, guys." I use my stern "boss" voice that they've hardly ever heard, making it clear that I'm not fooling around. "Now back to work and not another word about Isabelle or my bruises."

Here's to hoping their silence will last beyond Isabelle's visit.

TWENTY-EIGHT

Of Course They're Single

Isabelle

THE ATMOSPHERE IN this office is weird. From what I understand, Anita is the only woman, and that probably explains the lack of tact in the male colleagues. Simon told me about this once. That if you have too many men in a team, the general behavior will head straight into the gutter. And usually, a single woman won't be enough to even things out. You need at least two.

I've always worked in a female-heavy field so I haven't encountered the phenomenon first-hand before. It's kind of fascinating—because they're being silly and awkward and not aggressive or creepy. The stories Simon told me from his days in mechanical engineering unfortunately tended toward the second category.

"They're all single, aren't they?" I ask Anita. The girl is odd in her own ways but she catches on quick to everything I've told her this far, even though it's clear she's never set foot in a museum before. I don't think her dark eyes miss anything, including the fact that I'm glancing over at Thomas every ten seconds.

"Of course they're single." Anita scoffs. "They're geeks who haven't been exposed to women for years. They never get any practice except what they see on TV."

"Ah. Not the best reference, huh?"

"Not with what they're watching, no."

I decide to chance an almost-personal question. "There aren't *any* other women here?"

"Not on this team, no. There used to be two women in the team that's in the office across the hall. It's the same company but a different team, yeah? But they both quit within two months of each other last year." All of this is delivered without a single emotion showing on her smooth-skinned face. But I'm guessing the emotions are there. She's just really good at not showing them.

"That doesn't sound very good." If the only two women on a team leave close together, I'd be tempted to look to the rest of the team, and management, for explanations.

Anita shrugs. "The first one was snatched up by a competitor who could pay her a lot more than she got here. The second gave up when the male to female ratio went over critical mass. They're not bad people, but it takes a certain type of woman to withstand the idiotic jokes day in and day out."

"Yet you're still here."

A hint of a smile. "I wouldn't know what to do in a predominantly female environment. I'm good here. Besides, this team is more awkward, whereas the guys in the other team tend toward gross. I might not have stayed there either."

While Anita types in some of her notes on her laptop, I throw yet another glance toward Thomas. He's at his desk, staring angrily at his screen. I don't think he's actually seeing what's on the monitor, though. He's not typing, not clicking. I'd wager he's watching his two colleagues—the two who thought I was gorgeous—out of the corner of his eye.

"It's a bit weird to have a ten-person team and not one of them is in a relationship, isn't it?" Surely you can't hire people based on their marital status any more than you can based on their sex?

A one-shoulder shrug from Anita. "The married ones leave before the end of their trial period. There's only so much single-person talk they can take. Try to start a conversation on changing diapers with this lot and you'll understand."

I'm having a hard time visualizing Thomas in this odd environment. He seems like such a well-rounded person. "Is Thomas the one who hires new recruits?"

"He has been for the last year or so." Anita glances up at Thomas and their gazes meet. He seems worried. How did he know to look this way at that exact moment?

"He's learning the hard way that the family guys don't stay," Anita says. "Two married guys and one woman—she was single but, you know, female—have stayed for three months before very politely saying they've found something else, pack up, and leave."

"Did he hire you?"

"Yes. I was his first hire a little more than a year ago."

How odd. I've been attracted to Thomas from the first and it's not because of his looks. He's a genuinely nice guy who doesn't hold grudges and knows when to ask questions and when to shut up. His head is in the right place and I'd think he has the makings of a great boss. Why would so many of his colleagues leave? Can the rest of the team really be that bad?

If that's the case, why is *he* staying?

I study Anita and her expressionless face. "So why haven't you left?"

She looks away from what she's typing to meet my gaze. "Because I like it here. I don't mind the awkwardness and stupid questions. None of them would ever dare mess with me." She shoots another glance at Thomas. "Besides, he's a good boss. He gave me a chance without looking at my name or skin color. He doesn't treat me like just another Indian."

My breath stutters and I can't keep the surprise off my face. "What… What does 'treat you like another Indian' mean, exactly?"

"Assuming I'm stupid, that you have to explain everything to me step by step, that I can't think for myself." Still no emotion on her face, but she can't keep the anger and frustration out of her voice.

"I see." I don't know what else to say. I'll have to ask Simon if he has any experience with this. "Well, I've only known you for twenty minutes, but there's no way I'd assume you're stupid or slow. I can't wait to see the new version of the app when it's all in place."

"Yeah." She lights up a little. "These are great improvements. The category stuff shouldn't be too complicated to implement, either, so I hope I can include it in our next update." She glances in Thomas's direction, then back at me. "The part with different levels of information to access…that's going to take a little longer. It's quite the leap from what we have right now."

I laugh at her understatement. "The good thing about knowing what to improve is that you won't be sitting idle. Honestly, I have *so* many ideas for the information levels…" I sigh. "It's nice to feel useful again."

"You like giving away your time and expertise for free like this?" Anita smiles at me. An actual smile, with teeth and everything. She's stunning. "Will you please come back and go into more detail with me on the information stuff?"

"Well, I—"

"Also, Thomas is weird when you're here. I want to understand what's going on there. Are you two dating?" She gets a faraway look. "What happens if the boss leaves the ranks of the single?"

God, I can feel my blush lighting up my face. "We're not— I don't... What do you mean, he's weird?" He has seemed rather normal to me, except perhaps a little bit on edge with his two odd colleagues.

Anita indicates the two men who were bickering earlier. "It's the first time he's told them to shut it when they fantasize about those bruises, for one. He usually just lets them yap on, coming up with theories, each more stupid than the next."

"The bruises?"

"You didn't see them? He came back from a business trip four weeks ago with an enormous shiner on one eye. Refused to tell us what happened. Then, when it had almost faded—you know, he was down to green and yellow for the most part—he got a new one. I think that time he might have broken his nose. Still no explanation. And then less than a week ago, *another* shiner, although not so violent as the first. Benjamin and Clément have been trying to get him to spill the beans ever since. I think they secretly hope he's part of a fight club, that he's some badass by night pretending to be a geek by day."

I can't come up with a single thing to say. Why doesn't he want them to know what happened? He wasn't at fault in either of the three instances, simply an unlucky guy in the wrong place at the wrong time. Is it some sort of macho male thing? I never could understand that. Doesn't want to admit having been hit by a woman? But surely he could have told them he got punched without giving details on the who? Or would that also reflect badly on him somehow?

I'll have to ask Simon. He's a guy, he'll know, right?

"Hey, Thomas!" Anita yells, and I almost fall off my chair. "You should bring your girlfriend on as a consultant. I'm going to need to pick her brain for more than twenty minutes."

The two guys—Benjamin and Clément, if I'm not mistaken—snap their heads up, mouths open in surprise. "Girlfriend?" Clément says. "Boss, you failed to mention that when you made the introductions."

"She's *not* my girlfriend." Thomas's voice is harder than I've ever heard it. A boss's voice. That of someone who expects his orders to be followed.

Well, at least we're clear on that.

TWENTY-NINE

I Really Wanted It to Be the Monkey

Thomas

How DID I lose control of this situation so quickly?

Oh, right. I saw an opportunity to see Isabelle again and didn't stop to think that bringing her into my work environment wouldn't be the best idea.

We all put on different masks depending on the people around us. We're one person with our family. One when we're alone. A different one with our friends. And another at work. It's perfectly normal.

But most people apparently don't have problems when the different worlds mix. Friends coming over for dinner with the parents and their minds don't blank out because they don't know which version of themselves they're supposed to be.

The girl they have a crush on shows up at work and they don't turn into an emotionless jerk—to both the colleagues and the girl.

I learned the hard way that I needed an impenetrable mask in school, and subsequently, at work. If I was too close to the person I was at home or with my friends, I'd get hurt. Any weakness picked at. Any mistake paid for every single day for months on end. An open invitation for ridicule.

High school was torture. When I moved to Toulouse to study, I vowed never to find myself in a similar situation ever again. So I closed myself off from my classmates except for a select few that I trusted. I focused on the work, on getting everything right, and on becoming impenetrable. I learned how to get people to understand I wouldn't take a joke. They'd do better to take their fun elsewhere.

It has served me well. I have a job I love and a team that respects me—but doesn't really know me. Which is exactly how I want it.

I have a small group of close friends from my student days and we meet up regularly. *They* are allowed to make jokes, ridicule me, because I trust them. But they're the *only* ones.

As I watch Isabelle's face fall, I wonder if bringing her here is a decision I'll regret. Seems likely, honestly. She only knows the mask I wear with my friends. Not the partially closed-off Thomas with his family, and not the completely closed-off Thomas at work.

This is why I don't like discussing work with Vincent. It's difficult to talk about my day, being a different person when I'm with him.

It makes me see how robot-like I am when I'm at work.

Still, this is a lot worse than usual. I'm not a mean boss, or a particularly strict one. I just don't tell them anything personal, and don't expect them to tell me anything in return.

Anita putting the tag "girlfriend" on Isabelle has made my mind go all kamikaze. The guys knowing she's important to me is giving them ammunition.

On some level I realize it's stupid but I just can't expose myself like that.

After the first shock, Isabelle's face shuts down, making her eerily similar to Anita—who, for once, *is* showing emotion. And it's disappointment.

"Anita wasn't asking about your marital status," Isabelle says. She straightens in her seat and lifts her chin. "I wouldn't mind coming back to consult on the features of your app. But only if the boss approves, of course."

A small part of my brain is running around in circles, panicked at the idea of pushing Isabelle away. This guy isn't me, not really. Surely, she knows me well enough to realize what's going on here?

In any case, work-Thomas is firmly in charge in my head—I am at work, after all. "That sounds like a great idea, actually. Why don't you and Anita figure out how much time you'll need and I'll tell the HR department to add you to our payroll."

Hiring the woman I'm crushing on is *not* the best solution. It really isn't.

And yet, that's what happens.

"That'll work," Isabelle says and leans close to Anita to discuss, I assume, the details of their collaboration.

I'm left with Benjamin and Clément, who are staring at me like I've grown a second head, mouths open and shocked expressions on their faces. I'm tempted to snap at them, ask them what they're staring at, get them to go back to work.

But that would probably make things worse. Make them interested. Invite them to find a weakness. So I sit back down in my chair—when did I stand up?—and pretend to go back to work as if nothing out of the ordinary just happened.

Three minutes later, I'm convinced it worked. Until…

"I'm putting my money on the girlfriend hitting him. He tried to lay down the law like right now and she wasn't having it. That chick is a real firecracker."

I whip around so quickly my neck hurts. Benjamin isn't even looking at me. His eyes are on the code on his screen and he's tapping on his keyboard.

Clément, at his desk across from Benjamin, hums in agreement, but he's not looking away from his screen either. "I really wanted it to be the monkey, but I guess it's time to face facts. There's no way the boss is cool enough to have a pet monkey."

I don't know whether to cry or yell. Somehow, miraculously—probably because Isabelle is still here and I have a vague hope she still likes me—I do neither. "Will you guys *please* shut up about the shiners? Don't you have anything better to do?"

Clément looks up from his screen and meets my gaze. "Oh, you don't like it when we do that? It was just for fun, dude." He exchanges a quick glance with Benjamin. "Thought you liked it, honestly. Figured it was a chance to show off our level of imagination."

They really thought I liked it? What on earth gave them that impression?

The anger is winning out. I'm the *boss*, for crying out loud. They're not supposed to make fun of me. Who cares about imagination? Monkeys? I'll show them—

"I'll be back tomorrow." Isabelle is grabbing her things from my desk. I hadn't seen or heard her approach. "We'll do two-hour sessions in the morning every other day until we feel like we're done. Anita is confident she can keep up on the coding side of things, or at least specifying the features by the end of each day." She pauses, the first indication she's uncertain. "Thank you for this opportunity. It feels really good to be useful again."

My anger is long gone. My colleagues' insubordination insignificant. "I'm the one who should be thanking you, Isabelle. Your input is going to make our app a million times better. I'm… I'm sorry about just now. I don't…" I don't know what to say. I know something went wrong, but can't quite put my finger on it. I'd like nothing more than to blame everything on Benjamin and Clément, but an unsettling feeling in my gut tells me I'm to blame.

I just don't know why.

And I need to get Isabelle away from my office and my colleagues. The mixing of two worlds—or rather two me's—is wreaking havoc on my nerves.

"Can I accompany you downstairs?" It's more of a question than it should be. Benjamin, Clément, and Anita are all giving me odd looks.

Isabelle has turned into an ice queen. "If you wish." Without waiting, she turns on her heel and marches out of my office.

Benjamin whistles. "My money's on her."

I run after Isabelle.

THIRTY

Die Hard Idiocy

Isabelle

What the hell just happened?

One minute I'm enjoying myself, visualizing all the new features Anita and I can put together for their app, and the next Thomas is acting completely out of character, talking down to his colleagues, panicking when Anita assumed I'm his girlfriend—and doesn't *that* make me feel good about myself—and generally turning into a cold, emotionless asshole.

He just needs to tell me I'm stupid and I'd have a Pierre 2.0.

I storm out the door into the depressing hallway. The elevator doors open and a young woman of perhaps twenty, with golden hoop earrings and round gold-rimmed glasses, steps out. I brush past her, into the elevator, and push the button for the ground floor. Hard.

Thomas hesitates. Meets my gaze, gulps. And steps into the elevator.

I really wouldn't have minded if he'd stayed behind. "I'm capable of finding the door myself," I say, my tone so chilled I tug my scarf a little tighter around my neck.

"I'm really sorry," Thomas says as the doors slide shut. The elevator gives a jerk, then starts descending. "I behaved like a total asshole in there. You shouldn't have had to see that."

"I shouldn't have had to—" I throw my hands in the air in frustration. "If you're being a jerk you shouldn't worry about who sees it. You should worry about being a jerk! I cannot believe—"

The elevator stops.

The doors do not open.

Thomas sighs. Tries to look out through the minuscule crack in the elevator door. "We're between the ground floor and the first floor. As usual." With great resignation, he presses the call button on the control panel.

"We're stuck?" I know, stupid question. But I need to know for sure.

"Yeah. Don't worry, though. It won't last long. The contract stipulates they have to come within the hour." There's a ringing sound from the panel, and some static.

Ten seconds later, a woman greets us. Thomas greets her back and it becomes clear this is not his first time being stuck in here. He confirms the address, explains the situation, thanks the woman for her time, and says goodbye.

"That's it?" I ask. "Now what do we do?"

Thomas leans against the wall next to the control panel. "Now we wait. Unless you want to attempt some Die Hard idiocy and climb out of here?" He glances up at the hatch above us. "Clément tried that once. He got yelled at for over thirty minutes by the maintenance guys. And had to pay for the repairs to the stuff he broke on the way."

The walls had been feeling increasingly close, but Thomas's story gives me much-needed air. Focus on something else, not on the fact I'm stuck in here. "Why would he do that? Is he claustrophobic or something?"

The smile gracing Thomas's lips is sincere. "He had to pee. *Really* didn't want to do it in here with Anita watching."

A laugh bubbles out. "Oh, no!" I cover my mouth with one hand. "The poor guy. And Anita of all people."

"Yeah, she can be a little scary." Hands in pockets, Thomas lowers his gaze to his feet.

Is the normal Thomas back now? Is some distance from his office all it takes for the jerk to disappear? If the job makes him behave like that, why doesn't he find something else to do?

Is *this* the normal Thomas, or was the normal what I saw back with his colleagues? When is he pretending?

"Anita isn't scary," I say, my voice terser than I intended. "She's very bright and learns fast. *She* had good things to say about *you*."

His head whips up. "She did?" Sighing, he adjusts his stance. "I've never understood that girl. And I swear, whenever I look up, she's looking at me. She even did it when you were working with her! How does she ever get anything done? Does she not need to look at what she's doing?"

My laugh surprises me so much, it comes out close to a snort. Very elegant. "You think she's looking at you all the time? I can assure you that was not the case. You must somehow manage to both look up at the same time very often. It's the only explanation."

"But it's not just often, it's *all the time*!"

Another laugh escapes. I don't think he's joking around. He seems genuinely upset. "Or…maybe she's a sorceress."

Wide-eyed, Thomas stares at me for several beats, before cracking up, bending over, slapping his knee. "The fact that I seriously considered that a real possibility is frankly worrisome. Not sure if it says more about me or Anita."

"Well," I say, lifting my nose in the air and brushing imaginary lint from my shoulder. "Anita didn't seem to be overly focused on you, so I'm going to vote for you being the problem. Did *you* get anything done in the last hour? Or did you spend all your time staring at us and then blaming Anita for the times your eyes met?"

Smile gone now, Thomas straightens, and crosses his arms. Good old defensive stance. He doesn't look angry, though. More like defeated. Embarrassed.

"I was an idiot," he mumbles. "I'm really sorry. I don't do very well when my different worlds mix."

"Different worlds?"

His arms tighten, like he's trying to get free of bonds. "Workspace and private sphere. Never figured out how to mix them. Never wanted to."

"Huh." I'm not even sure I understand what he means. "Did you ever try?"

His blue eyes snap to meet mine. We're at opposite sides of the elevator but it feels like we're standing a lot closer than a couple of meters. "Try what?" he says.

"Mix your worlds. I won't pretend to understand what the problem is, but if it's turning you into a first-class jerk, maybe you should work on overcoming it."

His wince could be seen from outer space. "First-class jerk?"

"Yes." I sigh. "Well, I'll admit there are worse people out there. My ex-husband being one of them. But you were exhibiting the kind of behavior I usually see in people who aren't confident in their position of power, and talk down to everybody around them to establish their dominance. Where'd your sense of humor go?"

When Thomas doesn't say anything—and more importantly, doesn't seem to be angry about what I said—I continue. "I won't pretend to know you, Thomas. We've only hung out a couple of times, and our encounters seem to always end in violence." I spare a worried glance at the elevator doors. "But the violence has never been your doing. Not the actual violence, and not by provoking anyone to it. Overall, you've come across as a really great guy. Forgiving, with a sense of humor."

I think back to the time we've spent together in the past month, trying to find any hint of the kind of behavior Thomas exhibited with his colleagues.

The fact that I can't find any worries me. A lot.

I hadn't seen Pierre being a jerk coming either.

The walls start closing in on me again. How long since the call for help? I feel sweat forming on my back and remove my beret and scarf, hoping it will also help with getting more air into my lungs.

"Are you all right?" Thomas's voice sounds worried, and a little tinny. That can't be a good sign.

I open the top button of my coat and retreat to the corner of the elevator, leaning on the walls to stay upright. I can't quite figure out how to form a reply.

"Are you claustrophobic? Come, let me help you—"

"Don't!" My yell is probably heard throughout the building. Full-on panic. "Stay away from me."

Thomas retreats to the opposite corner, his expression scared and wary. Hands up to show he means no harm.

I find it a little easier to breathe. "I'm fine," I say, despite a lot of proof to the contrary. "But, please, just…stay over there, okay?"

THIRTY-ONE

I Look Forward to Our Collaboration

Thomas

I DON'T THINK I could have messed this up any more if I tried.

The woman I like saw the person I am when I'm at the office and didn't like what she saw. My colleagues saw hints of the guy I am outside of the office and started asking a ton of questions I don't want to answer. I got stuck in our cursed elevator and now Isabelle is freaking out—obviously because of something I did or said.

"I'm so sorry," I say, keeping my voice low and calm. "I didn't mean to scare you." I hang my head. "I never should have invited you here."

"Why?" Isabelle's expression is close to a sneer. "So I wouldn't see this side of you until it was too late?"

"What? No!" I run a hand through my hair as I search for the right words. "I never wanted you to see this side of me."

"Oh." Isabelle scoffs. "That's *so* much better. "What she doesn't know can't hurt her, is that it?"

I frown as I struggle to keep up. "It's not a question of hurting you or not. It's more…a need to know thing? If you're part of my personal sphere, you don't need to know the professional me."

"I don't know what your definition of professional is, but what I saw in there." She points upward, in the direction of my office. "That wasn't professional."

Ouch. I'm not about to get into an argument with her on the subject, though. I guess we'll just have to agree to disagree.

"Why invite me to work with Anita if you don't want to mix your 'spheres'?" The air quotes she makes with her hands carry a hefty dose of sarcasm.

"Because I wasn't thinking." And isn't that the truth. Whenever Isabelle is around, all logical thought goes right out the window. I didn't stop to think about the impact on my own mental stability if Isabelle came to the office on a regular basis. I just jumped at the opportunity to meet her again.

I get the feeling I'll always jump at the opportunity to spend time with this woman.

Isabelle comes very close to rolling her eyes at me. "So I *shouldn't* come back in two days, like we planned? You'll explain to Anita that it's your fault and that I'm not the one leaving her in the lurch?"

"Uh…" Is that what I want? The two sides of me are warring inside my head. One part wants her to come back as often as possible, however possible. The other wants to keep her far away from my office and my colleagues.

If she comes here on a regular basis, she's either going to be too disgusted by what she sees and go away forever, or I won't be able to keep the office mask on when she's near and everything I've worked on since high school can come crashing down around me.

"Maybe it is for the best if you don't come here anymore," I say hesitantly. I light up as an idea forms. "Maybe you could consult on the phone? Or via video conference?"

The disdain on Isabelle's beautiful features is like a knife to the heart. "*That's* the solution you come up with? Really?"

"What?" I throw out my arms. "It would allow for you to participate without us creating this kind of situation again. I got the feeling you *wanted* to be involved? If that's not the case, I'm sure we can find someone else to work with Anita for a couple of days."

Isabelle stares at me for several moments. She opens her mouth to say something three times, closes it again as she changes her mind.

I wish I understood what's going on in her head. Surely, we can find a solution that suits the both of us? And go back to getting along so well? I need for the anger, the fear, and the disdain on her face to go away, and sooner rather than later. I want the smiles, the joy, and the humor to come back.

"I can't believe you're really this clueless," Isabelle whispers. "I thought *I* needed work, but this is something else." All emotion flees her face, be it positive or negative. A cold mask is all that's left.

"I'll be coming back in two days to meet with Anita, and as many times after that as it requires for her to make your app viable." She cuts me off with a look when I open my mouth to speak. "I intend to keep my promise to Anita. And I won't be relegated to phone calls because you're too much of a coward to be yourself in front of your colleagues. Or in front of me. I have no idea which Thomas is the real one."

"I'm the real me when I'm with—"

Isabelle holds up a hand. "Don't. Just don't. I don't want to hear it. I have enough on my plate right now and have no intention of taking on your double-personality tendencies on top of everything else. Until you figure yourself out, I think it's best if we keep our relationship purely professional."

I've seen this look on her face before. Once.

When she told her ex-husband in no uncertain terms that the "ex" was a permanent fixture.

And now, the same applies to me. Except I don't really have a status to attach the ex to. Maybe friend? Who hoped for more.

I search for something to say to make her change her mind. I come up short. She doesn't want to stay away from my office. In fact, she's made it very clear that Anita and the app are more important than me and my comfort zone. And she doesn't want to hear me tell her I'm the real me when I'm with her.

The elevator doors slide open a few centimeters.

A green eye appears on a level with the elevator floor. "You guys all right in there?"

"We're fine," I say, happy my voice sounds close to normal. "Happy to see you again, Didier."

"Thomas! Long time, no see!"

I sigh. "Yeah. I've been taking the stairs lately, for some reason."

"Smart man." The eye moves to take in the rest of the elevator. "Ah, I see," he says when he spots Isabelle. "Are the both of you all right with a meter-high jump to get out or should I go up to the top floor to pull you up to the first floor with the crank?"

Isabelle catches on quickly. "We can jump."

Five minutes later, Didier and his colleague have the elevator door open and secured. The bottom half opens to the ground floor lobby, the top on nothing but concrete.

Didier offers his hand to Isabelle when she moves to jump down and she accepts it. I make the jump without help—this is not my first time.

"You think we'll ever have an elevator that works all days of the week?" I ask in an attempt at humor that falls completely flat.

"We'll look around, as usual," Didier replies. "But chances of us finding anything new aren't great."

Nodding, I leave Didier and his colleague to their job of freeing up the elevator and getting it back up and running—for a few hours, at least.

I run toward the front door when I see Isabelle pulling her black beret down over her ears, her red scarf already wound around her neck.

I don't *think* she'd leave without so much as a goodbye. But I'm not confident enough to put it to the test.

When the door opens, her gaze snaps to mine. Still cold. Distant.

"Tell Anita I'll be back in two days like we planned," she says. "I look forward to our collaboration."

Before I can get out a single word, she leaves.

I stand there shivering in nothing but my shirt in the cold March afternoon, watching her retreating back until she disappears into the metro station at Jean Jaurès.

She never looks back.

THIRTY-TWO

Maybe Chamomile Can Help

Isabelle

My head feels like lead. I can barely keep my eyes open. It's a good thing I'm on foot or getting home from my therapist's office might have been downright dangerous. The half-hour walk has helped air things out a little but not enough for me to be functional for the rest of the day.

I've spent an hour and a half with my therapist, looking at moving lights and working through some of my roughest memories of my time with Pierre. At the beginning, the therapist's method seemed honestly weird, but I was willing to give it a go. And after my second session, I can confirm it's working.

I can see the manipulations Pierre subjected me to, know it wasn't right of him to do that, and know he hurt me—but not actually feel the hurt anymore. It's like I used to have an open wound that I'd try to cover up with band-aids only to rip it open every time something made me think of my ex-husband, but now it has scarred over. I can see where I was hurt, I can remember how much it did hurt, but it's not painful any longer. Poking it won't make me go crazy.

But the method comes at a price. The energy my brain has expended on working through those memories must be formidable. When I get home, I'm going straight to bed and expect my nap to last at least two hours. Last week I was so conked out, I thought I was back in England when I woke up.

When I reach my parents' home, I find Simon sitting on the front stairs. He's having as much trouble as me with adapting to living with our folks, and he's taken to spending time out here, to "get some fresh air." When he comes back in, he's usually ice cold.

"Hey, Isa," he says as I come through the gate. "How'd it go?" He gets a good look at my face. "That bad, huh?"

"It's not bad." I throw myself down on the stairs next to him and lean my head on his shoulders. Ever since his growth spurt at seventeen, this has been one of my favorite spots for resting my head. "In fact, it's good. Just...exhausting."

Simon nods. He's been extremely helpful and solicitous since I came home, being there for me at every turn. But something is bothering him, and it's getting worse. And he still won't tell me about it. He claims he wants me to focus on me right now, that I don't need to be burdened with his problems, but I'm not buying it. He's keeping a secret from me and I don't know if the good sisterly thing to do is to let him keep it, or to force it out of him.

"And how are you feeling about meeting Thomas when you work with Anita tomorrow?"

I groan. "I'm going to have to apologize to him." See, that's the bad thing about good therapy. It makes you realize when you've overreacted.

This doesn't absolve Thomas of the crap he pulled, not by a long shot. But one wrong doesn't justify another. His behavior in the office and the elevator that day reminded me of Pierre, and that freaked me out. Made me go into full survival mode and defend myself as best I could—which happened to be walking away.

I've been back in his office twice since then, and both times Anita has been the one to come get me at the door and to escort me out after. Thomas has been there, sitting at his corner desk and pretending to be absorbed by whatever's on his screen, and hasn't said a word to me. He's not fooling anyone, of course, including his not-so-bright colleagues, who seem to have set up a bet on which of us will fold first.

Thomas ignores them, apparently believing that tactic will get them to stop.

I'm going to have to let whoever has tomorrow down, win, because I can't live with myself if I don't apologize to Thomas and explain why I reacted like I did. Once that's out, I can get on with my life.

A life without Thomas, unfortunately.

I did overreact, but that doesn't mean his behavior was good. It certainly isn't good for me. Too close to Pierre, which is a type of person I've already proved I can't survive with.

I may make mistakes from time to time, but at least I learn from them.

We sit in silence for a while. I doze on Simon's shoulder, feeling perfectly safe and content, until I start losing feeling in my toes because of the cold. "I'm going inside," I tell Simon. "I might look at some apartment listings before I take a nap. Should I look for one or two bedrooms?"

We've both concluded we've had our share of time in our childhood home and need to get back to leading our own, adult lives. Working with Anita on the app has been great for me, and I'm thrilled to be back in Toulouse again, so I've decided to stay. At least for a while. Until I figure out what I want—which isn't going to happen under Maman's watchful eye.

Simon has told me he's also moving out, but not where to.

Now he hangs his head and gives such a heartfelt sigh, I instinctively reach out to give him a hug. "Go with one bedroom," he murmurs. "I'm gonna have to get back at some point." I don't get a single word out before he adds, "I'll tell you about it once I've figured things out, Isa. Promise. But I'm not going to figure it out until I go back to Perpignan."

I push to my feet. "Do you have to be so cryptic when I already have a headache?"

I go inside and settle into the couch closest to the large radiator, covered in three blankets. I prepare a cup of herbal tea and flip open my laptop, typing in my apartment research.

"How was your therapy session?" Maman comes in from the downstairs office, empty coffee cup in hand.

"It was good. Thank you for giving me her number." Nice and polite. That's about as warm and cozy as it ever gets with my mother.

Maman nods as she puts the cup in the dishwasher. "She helped me a great deal some years ago. I'm glad it's working out for you."

"She— You... *You* went to therapy?" My hand is frozen over the keyboard and it's possible my mouth is hanging open.

The flat stare Maman gives me makes me cringe inside. It means a criticism is coming. I'll never be good enough for her.

"Why is it so surprising I've been to therapy?" she says, leaning against the kitchen counter. "It's much more common than you apparently think. You don't need to wait for a complete breakdown before seeing one. In fact, you *shouldn't*."

Yep, definitely an Isabelle-is-too-stupid-for-this-world moment. But I'm too curious to cut my losses here. "But...why?"

"Why I went to therapy?" Maman shrugs and glances out the kitchen window. "Some issues at work I had trouble processing in a constructive manner. The therapist helped me put things in perspective and stop beating myself up about things I had no control over."

I let out an actual squeak. "Beating yourself up?" Is that even possible? Maman never hesitates about anything. She has all the answers, lays down all the rules.

I expect a biting response. Instead I get a long sigh. "Yes, Isabelle. I have doubts just like everybody else. But I never showed you that side of me, did I?"

Shaking my head, I wonder what is happening. Is it possible I've walked into an alternate dimension?

"Parents always do their best to protect their children," Maman says softly. "Including protection from their own faults and weaknesses. If I was upset about something at work, or when Mamie had to be moved to a retirement home, or when Papa almost lost his job—"

"Papa almost lost his job? When?" Why didn't I hear of this?

"Relax, Isabelle. He's not about to lose his job. This was twenty years ago. And my point is that we didn't tell you about it because we didn't want to scare you." Her lips lift into an almost-smile. "Fifteen seemed to be difficult enough as it was."

Wasn't that the truth. But still... Why keep the family drama from me? Did they really think I was that weak?

"We didn't want to worry you, so we never told you. I still think it was the right decision for that particular case, but I'm starting to realize we protected you from *everything*, to the point where we didn't tell you about our lives outside of this house at all."

"I don't—" I stop short as I realize something. "I know *nothing* about your lives outside of the family sphere." How is that even possible? I spent eighteen years living under the same roof as Maman and Papa, and I have no idea what they're like at work, or when they're out with friends? Hell, I don't even know if they have friends.

The smile Maman gives me is a little sad, an emotion I can't recollect seeing on her features before. "Don't worry about it, Isabelle, it's not your fault. It's ours."

"But I should have, I don't know, at least asked you how your day was from time to time!" Oh my God, I've never asked my parents how they were doing. The discussion was always a one-way street. And I never questioned it.

"I might not even have answered you honestly back then," Maman says. "I discussed several issues with the therapist when I went to see her. I started out because I had problems at work, but it quickly veered over to more personal territory. I expended far too much energy on keeping you and your brother safe from my emotions. I never would have let my guard down back then." The eyes that look so much like my own shine with hope. "But I would now."

The world really is full of wonders. I hope for my brother to open up and my mother does it instead.

I realize my herbal tea has gone cold in my hand but still take a sip. Maybe chamomile can help when the world has spun off its axis.

I can't help but wonder if this is a setup. If I take her up on her invitation, will it spring the trap and bring another load of hurt?

"You always made me feel like I wasn't good enough." I blurt the words out. I set my laptop down on the couch because I'm feeling jerky and don't want it to end up on the floor.

"I know." Maman's voice breaks on the last word.

Are those tears forming in her eyes?

Abort! Abort!

But it's too late. As the first tear falls, she starts talking. "I only ever wanted to help you, Isabelle. Simon, too. If there was a mistake in your homework, I wanted to help you to get it right, so you'd get good grades and the possibility of living a happy life. If you weren't the fastest on the track team, I pointed out the areas needing improvement because I wanted to help. *Not* because I thought you were a failure or because I only saw the faults. I've always been so proud of you both. And it pains me to see you suffer now and not knowing how to help. I'm *afraid* to help because I've realized my helping did more harm than good when you were young."

I'm holding it together only because I don't want to spill tea all over myself. The words coming out of my mother's mouth are the ones I've always needed to hear, but never thought I'd get. Maman *isn't* a robot?

She's proud of me?

"My life's a mess," I say.

"Your life is finally on the right track, *chérie*. You stood up to that idiot you married, you're on your way to finding a new career here in Toulouse. You've met a new man…?"

The laugh bursting out of me is as inelegant as they come. "Subtle, Maman."

Maman smiles. "He seems nice. When he's not bleeding all over my pajamas."

"He was nice. Then he wasn't anymore." I take a sip of my cold tea. "So, tell me, how was your day?"

For the first time ever, Maman tells me about her day at work.

THIRTY-THREE

A Six-Pack of Beer and My Favorite Pizza

Thomas

Turns out I'm an idiot.

After Isabelle's first visit to my office, I was in a foul mood. I hadn't behaved in the best manner, but I did apologize, and even explain why I'd been so weird in front of my colleagues. I never tell *anyone* about that.

I made an exception for her, and she threw it in my face.

So that night, I broke the rule again, this time with Vincent.

I told him about Isabelle's disastrous visit to our offices, about our fight, and thereby about me being a different person at work and with friends. Seriously, *everybody* behaves differently at work and at home.

Except, apparently, not to the extent I take it.

"I always thought you were weird not to talk about work with me, dude," Vincent said. "I figured you wanted to think about something else for a while, not that you're actually two different people and have trouble dividing the world up along the same clearly delineated lines you've created in your mind."

So I got mad again. My turn to walk out without so much as a goodbye.

Luckily, Vincent is a real friend, much better than I deserve. He showed up on my doorstep the next day, came straight over from work, with a six-pack of beer and my favorite pizza. "Wanna try again?"

With one more day of stewing under my belt, I was starting to see reason. Or rather, realize maybe my way of doing things wasn't the only way, and this might be why other people made new friends at work and I never did.

That slight opening was all Vincent needed to crack me wide open. He questioned me through most of the evening and halfway through the night, identifying every behavior he tagged as "not normal" and going through about a million explanations and proofs why that was. I argued back to the best of my ability—and I'm *good* in an argument—but I couldn't win a single point. Some took me hours to concede, some minutes.

Toward the end, I didn't even bother arguing anymore. I heard the problems the moment they were out of my mouth.

So, yeah, I'm damaged goods because I was bullied in high school.

And although there's no chance of Isabelle liking me again—dissecting my discussion with her in detail with Vincent helped me see she must have had some serious ex-husband flashbacks with how I was behaving—I must at least apologize.

Properly this time. For the right things.

Maybe we can at least be friendly when she drops by for her meetings with Anita.

Isabelle is scheduled to come at two. Today. With ten minutes on the clock, I don't stand a chance of doing anything remotely intelligent, so I arrange the pastries I bought during my lunch break on a platter and make sure the extra mugs in our kitchenette are clean in case Isabelle wants coffee.

When I start cleaning up the desks of the two colleagues who are absent today, Benjamin raises a hand, like he's a six-year-old with a question. "Dude, what's going on? You walk into another door and hit your head for real this time?"

I don't answer. I realize this is one of the situations Vincent qualified as not normal.

Yeah, he was right. Nobody else I know would react to a joke by turning cold and ignoring the person making the joke. Not even at work. They'd either laugh and go along with the joke, or make it clear they didn't think it was funny. Me not reacting at all seems to be a defense mechanism to avoid judgment and ridicule, no matter what direction it might be coming from.

How did I never notice this before?

Luckily, I don't get any time to ponder the question, because Isabelle walks through the door. She's wearing the same black beret and red scarf, and she's added a touch of matching red lipstick.

She's gorgeous.

Despite knowing better, my heart beats faster and hopes there's a chance she'll forgive me and will maybe want to kiss me again.

I move forward with the intention of intercepting her before she makes it to Anita's desk. If I wait until they're done, I'll lose my nerve.

But Isabelle doesn't follow Anita like she's done every other time she's been here. She doesn't look away from me, pretending I'm not here.

She comes right at me.

We meet in the middle, next to Clément's desk. Clément looks up at Isabelle. Starts smiling. Looks at my probably murderous frown. Stops smiling. He turns back to his screen and pretends to go back to work.

I happen to see he's clicking on an empty spot on his desktop.

"Thomas," Isabelle says, her voice not exactly warm and friendly, but a far stretch from the distant cold I've been treated to since our fight. "I was wondering if I might have a word?"

A weird sound comes from Clément but he's smart enough not to look up.

"I'd love that," I say. "I mean, yes, of course. Uh…" God, I'm botching this up completely. I can't find my words, my mind's scrambled, and I'm visualizing pulling a cartoonish heart out of my chest and laying it at Isabelle's feet.

I have to apologize before I chicken out. I don't know what she's planning to say to me, but if it is to tell me this is her last visit and I'll never see her again, I won't have the courage to say what I need to say.

"Actually, I have something I need to tell you, too." I take one step back and hold out my arm in invitation toward our kitchen area. "I bought some pastries. Would you like a *chocolatine*? Or perhaps a croissant? I also have coffee," I add desperately when Isabelle seems to hesitate and not in a would-that-be-polite kind of way.

She really is going to break it off completely, and she doesn't want the snacks because it's a sort of acceptance of hospitality.

"Please?" I'm not beyond a little begging.

And although I'm watching Isabelle for any hint of what she's thinking, I catch Clément in my peripheral vision, stretching his neck to stare at me over his screen with a shocked expression.

"I'm definitely voting for having walked into a door," Benjamin says from behind me. "Or maybe a wall. The boss is broken."

I'm so very tempted to bring Isabelle away from my colleagues. Out to the hallway, or outside, or across town… I *really* don't want them to be here when I apologize to Isabelle. They could *learn* something about me.

Which is why I *have* to do it here.

"I never walked into any doors," I say, my eyes still on Isabelle. "I was punched."

Complete silence.

"Oh, wait." I swivel to meet a shocked Benjamin's gaze. "That was the first time. The second time I was head-butted in the nose." When I find that the way Benjamin's eyebrows are disappearing into his messy hair quite satisfying, I figure I might as well go for broke. "The third time, I was hit again. Not sure it qualifies as a punch, though. The guy clearly didn't know what he was doing."

Clément's voice is about an octave higher than usual. "But the first two did?"

Isabelle, I'm happy to note, seems to be enjoying the banter. She's smiling and some of the worry lines she's had every time she came here over the past two weeks are smoothing out.

I'm looking at her as I answer Clément. "Oh, the first one definitely did. Same person who made the punch and the head-butt."

Clément whistles. "You must have seriously pissed him off, dude. What'd you do?"

I shove my hands in my pocket and cock my head as I pretend to ponder a question. "Everybody always assumes it's a guy. I can't quite decide if that's sexist, or realistic, or what."

"Dude!" Benjamin yells so loudly, Isabelle startles. "You were hit by a *girl?*"

Yeah, that's *exactly* the reaction I expected.

But my own reaction isn't. I'm not embarrassed, I'm not afraid they'll bully me for it. I've known these people for over two years. We've spent an ungodly amount of time together if you sit down and count the hours.

Clément and Benjamin won't bully me. Tease me, yes. But that's a *good* thing. It means I'm part of the group.

I think I'm grinning like a maniac. I'm feeling so light I hardly know what to do with myself, almost jumping from foot to foot.

"I don't think *girl* is the right word," I say. "I mean, she's not old or anything, but definitely beyond girl."

Everybody starts as Anita speaks up for the first time, from across the room. "It was Isabelle, wasn't it? You did something stupid and she hit you."

I'm not going to answer that. I'll own up to being hit by a woman, but I'll not tell them it was Isabelle. That would have to come from her. However… "Why does *everyone* assume I did something stupid to deserve being hit?"

"That seems like the logical explanation." Clément is dead serious.

I purse my lips. "I guess that third time, you *could* say I did something stupid. The guy saw me kissing his ex-wife. So it's understandable he'd be mad. But that does *not* mean I deserved it. Even if it was a weak punch."

Benjamin whoops. "The boss has a girlfriend! That why you bought pastries?"

"The pastries were for Isabelle, idiot," Clément says absently, his eyes going from Isabelle, to me, and back again.

"I, uh…" I send a worried glance at Isabelle. "I didn't say I have a girlfriend. I don't."

Anita has left her desk and walks up to stand next to Isabelle.

Bumping shoulders, she says, "So? Did you hit Thomas? What did he do?"

Isabelle's hand rises to cover her mouth. But her eyes are smiling and I think she's holding back a laugh. She takes a deep breath. "He woke me up because he had to pee and I punched him."

THIRTY-FOUR

Who Wins the Bet?

Isabelle

SINCE WHEN AM I proud of punching people in the face for no valid reason? Because pride is definitely the feeling filling my chest right now. I'm grinning like a fool, enjoying far too much the shock on Clément and Benjamin's faces.

"Why…" Clément gapes at Thomas. "Why would you need to wake her up to go pee? That's the weirdest—"

"We were on a plane!" Thomas isn't having any more luck than me at keeping the laughter back. "I had the window seat, she was on the aisle, and she'd fallen asleep before we even took off! It was torture."

"Oh." Clément deflates a little in his seat. "That makes more sense."

"What about the head-butting two weeks later?" Benjamin asks. "That wasn't you, too, was it?"

Now I'm giggling. I think it's a nervous reaction. Should I be worried I apparently take pleasure in telling people of my violent exploits?

"No, that was me, too." My voice is higher than ever and I let out a sort of whine like a balloon deflating as I fight valiantly not to laugh. "He went in for *la bise*, I misunderstood, backed up, and bounced right off my brother's shoulder and into Thomas's nose." I meet Thomas's eyes, making sure he sees the apology there. "It was *awful*."

"Don't worry about it," Thomas says kindly. "It gave these guys something to talk about for weeks, if not months. Right, guys?"

Benjamin's mouth snaps shut. "Well, we won't be wagering on what happened anymore, that's for sure. Who wins the bet, anyway?"

"I'm not sure if anyone had 'head-butted by girlfriend when he got too close.'" Clément opens a drawer and searches through the mess inside. "Let me get the tracking sheet."

"I think we'll leave you to it," Thomas says and once again invites me to come with him to the kitchen area. "How about that coffee?"

Feeling much lighter, I smile and nod. "Coffee sounds good. And I think you mentioned *chocolatines*?"

When we're in the tiny kitchenette in the corner, Thomas takes a clean mug from the cupboard and pours me a coffee. "Here. It's not the most fancy coffee you'll ever have, but it's fresh." He keeps his voice low and with both of us turning our backs on the rest of the office, nobody should be able to overhear. It's as private as it can get in an open plan office like this.

My joy dims slightly as I take a deep breath and prepare to do what I came here for—apologize. It's not going to be fun, but I have to get it over with so I can move on with my life without coming back to a moment I regret every time something vaguely similar happens.

"I have something I need to say. About our fight. I—"

"I'm really sorry I behaved like an ass." Thomas doesn't even let me finish. The laughter is gone, and anxiety seems to have taken its place. His blue eyes are serious and sincere and he seems short of breath. "I have to get this out now, or I'm not sure if I'll work up the courage again."

Slightly off-kilter because I was interrupted just as *I* was going to apologize, I'm not sure what to say.

"I behaved like a complete jerk," Thomas says, talking fast. "I completely understand if you don't want anything to do with me ever again, especially because of your past with Pierre, but I have to at least apologize properly. *Chocolatine?*" He holds one of the pastries out to me and I mechanically accept it.

He's not expecting me to eat right now, is he?

"Sorry, I'm really nervous."

Yeah, I can tell.

"Look. My friend Vincent has hounded me relentlessly because of how I behaved during our fight. Because I'm the *reason* there was a fight. It was a bit of a process, but I've come to understand that my being a different person at work and at home wasn't quite normal."

"Normal."

His oh-so-sincere blue eyes hold mine to the point where I'm not sure I'd notice if a fight erupted behind us. "I told you I was bullied in high school, right? Well, it turns out that had more of an impact on the way I've lived my life than I realized. Because although everyone is slightly different at work—you know, less swearing, no inappropriate jokes, all very above-board—I appear to have taken it to a whole other level."

He throws a quick glance at his colleagues, who are all leaning over Clément's desk, presumably trying to figure out who won the bet on the cause of his black eyes. "I never shared anything about myself with these people. I was afraid they'd use it against me." A frown line appears between his brows. "And now that Vincent has pointed it out to me, it seems very stupid."

"I've never gotten the feeling any of your colleagues mean you any harm." It's the only thing I can think of saying.

"And they don't." Thomas lets out a heavy sigh. "But it's probably going to take me a while to completely accept it. It's like a knee-jerk reaction telling me to never give anyone ammunition against me."

Thomas tries to grab my hand. I appreciate the sentiment, he's being very sincere. But my problem is I have a mug of coffee in one hand and a *chocolatine* in the other. I haven't tasted either.

I place both items on the counter, give a regretful sigh at the delicious odors wafting up, and take Thomas's hands in mine. "Thank you for telling me this. It does help to understand where you were coming from. And I guess I see the similarities with Pierre that made me react the way I did."

Thomas opens his mouth to object, but I squeeze his hand. "You've made your apology. Now let me make mine."

His mouth snaps shut and he gives my hands a squeeze.

"Like I just said, your behavior reminded me of Pierre. Which brings out *my* automatic reflexes. And much like you, I didn't realize it at the time. I simply reacted. When I *did* realize, I was horrified. I will not let Pierre influence my life when he's no longer a part of it.

"So I've been working with a therapist, and it's been a great help. But in order to really put it in the past, I have to properly apologize to you. You shouldn't have to pay for Pierre's sins."

"But—" Thomas clears his throat. "But I did behave terribly. I was rude and dismissive and you shouldn't have to endure such behavior, with or without the awful ex-husband."

Warmth spreads in my chest at the obvious sincerity behind his words. This is nothing like dealing with Pierre, who could never own up to any shortcoming or mistake. Their difference in treating the backlash of their mistakes couldn't be bigger—a fact that makes something settle into place in my heart, letting me breathe a little easier.

"Your behavior was far from perfect." I give his hands a squeeze and take half a step closer so the tips of my boots touch his shoes. "But everybody makes mistakes from time to time. The important part is recognizing it and being ready to work on doing better the next time."

I look over his shoulder at his colleagues. Six of them crowded around Clément's desk, ostensibly discussing the bet, but clearly keeping an eye on us. The guys seem to be poking fun at their boss, standing there in the kitchen area holding hands with a woman—but in a good way. These aren't kindergartners who think girl cooties are horrible. They're guys who love to poke fun at their friends—to show support. Anita is standing slightly apart from the rest of the group, not even pretending not to stare at us. When our eyes meet, she winks and gives a thumbs up.

Okay then.

"If I understand where your issue stems from," I say. "You've already gone ahead and proved you could do better the next time, haven't you? Tell me, how hard was it to admit you'd been punched by a girl?"

"Woman." His blue eyes shine and he smiles wide enough for his crooked tooth to poke out. "You're definitely not a girl." He licks his lips. "And it wasn't as hard as I expected it to be.

Although I'm becoming hyper-aware of the way they're staring at us right now."

I shrug. "From what I understand, they have two years of catching up to do. It'll calm down in a bit."

"I was punched by a woman by mistake, then head-butted in the nose, again by mistake, then awkwardly hit by the ex-husband of the woman I kissed. This isn't going to calm down anytime soon."

I let out a peal of laughter. "Well, I hope I'll get to witness some of it first hand while I'm working with Anita. They won't be able to keep quiet for several hours, will they?"

Thomas hangs his head. "They most definitely won't. God, I hope I won't regret this."

I think the next words to come out of my mouth surprise me more than they do Thomas. I came here with the intention of apologizing and then telling Thomas we wouldn't be seeing each other outside of a professional setting. I wouldn't run the risk of ending up with someone like Pierre again.

Except he's nothing like Pierre. Not in the way that's important, anyway.

So I grab my coffee and my *chocolatine* and move toward Anita's desk across the room. "Why don't we have dinner tonight? You can tell me all about the torture they put you through and I'll repeat whatever Anita will tell me while you can't hear."

With an assurance I wasn't aware I had, I don't even wait for an answer before walking away.

THIRTY-FIVE

A Fully Functional Surveillance Camera

Thomas

This afternoon is the longest I've ever had to live through at work.

Isabelle stays with Anita for two hours. They're clearly working—I can see the notes popping up on our virtual idea board as they create them—but I'm pretty sure they're also discussing me. Or my relationship with Isabelle. Or both. Or is this just me being my usual paranoid self? And if they *are* discussing me, what are they saying? Neither of them have been sending me dirty looks, so that's a good sign, right?

When I'm not preoccupied with the women, the men take over. This is the stuff I was really worried about, the part making my old bully victim wounds rip open. Will the guys still accept me if they get to know the real me? The not-so-serious and not always confident me? The man who manages to get hit twice by a woman and still fall for her?

If I look at it rationally, I think I'm good. Both Clément and Benjamin keep ribbing me throughout the afternoon, but it's all in good cheer. Some of the other colleagues, the ones who don't usually dare talk to or about me on anything but work, even add a comment or two. There's no criticism, no jeering, no meanness. Only good-natured teasing.

But I'm very much aware of the irrational part of my brain, and it's is not as confident. What if the guys are just prepping me, making me grow complacent so I give up even more details about my life, only to come back with an even stronger attack later? What if they're pretending to like me, and when I'm no longer around to overhear, they'll laugh about me among themselves?

I *know* it's irrational. But that doesn't stop the thoughts from forming.

Maybe I should look into getting a therapist. It seems to be working for Isabelle. And the fact the scared part of my brain doesn't want to go probably means it's a good idea.

First things first, though: dinner with Isabelle tonight.

I didn't imagine that, right? She asked me to dinner. Tonight. I'm pretty sure it's not just a way to let me down easy, but with my mind running in circles, I can't figure out up from down.

Somehow, I survive until it's time for Isabelle to leave. Instead of walking the most direct route from Anita's desk to the door, she comes down to my corner, a gentle smile playing on her lips.

"Anita tells me you don't *have* to stay until six every night, that it's only mandatory until four thirty?" She makes a show of looking at her watch. "Oh, look! It's four thirty-five."

I sit there, gaping like a fish out of water.

Clément and Benjamin roar with laughter—but even I can recognize it's in a good way, nothing mean. "You're no use to us today, anyway, boss! Go with your girlfriend."

It kicks me out of my stupor. I'm about to correct them and say Isabelle isn't my girlfriend—not yet, but a man can hope—when I realize it will simply bring on a conversation I'm not ready to have, and certainly not with an audience.

"I think I *will* leave early today," I say with as much pride as I can muster. "Let me grab my things and I'll join you by the door. We're *not* taking the elevator down."

Isabelle giggles and my insides dance a jig. "Don't you want to be stuck in a small space with me, Thomas?"

Is she flirting with me? Does this qualify as flirting? Or just banter?

Why am I too awkward to know the difference?

"That elevator breaks down several times a week," Clément says. "But has a fully functional surveillance camera. Just saying, in case you want to live dangerously."

Isabelle's eyebrows have gone into her hairline. "Well, now I certainly don't want to."

"Shouldn't have said anything, Clément," Benjamin yells from the printer across the room. "We could have asked the security team for the tape after."

Okay, time to go.

I grab a laughing Isabelle and push her toward the door, saying quick goodbyes to everyone on the way. She seems to be having fun but if the guys take the jokes any further into the gutter, I'm not sure she'll ever want to come back.

"Simon told me about this," Isabelle says, a little short of breath as we reach the hallway outside the office. "The guys making dirty jokes and stuff when there aren't enough women on the team. It's *fascinating* to see in real life."

"You make us sound like zoo animals," I say as I hold open the door to the stairwell. "Wanna bring a taxidermist next week and have us all set up in an action scene to your liking?"

As the words come out of my mouth, my mind comes up with an idea for a scene, proving I'm as far down into the gutter as my colleagues. Possibly further.

Something must have shown on my face because Isabelle stops on the stairs, laughing so hard she has to hold onto the handrail to keep from falling.

And I'm *happy* to have made a fool of myself if it can get such a reaction out of her. Guess there's a first time for everything.

Once we're out on the sidewalk, we both stop, and look at each other.

Now what? Isabelle wanted us to have dinner together but it's not even five o'clock. The restaurants won't open until three hours from now.

"I wish they left the Christmas decorations up through the winter," Isabelle says on a dreamy sigh. "I just love strolling through the city and watching the lights. This avenue is usually covered with lights, right?"

"Yes, although it's a bit too wide and open for my tastes. I prefer the narrow streets closer to the Capitole." I'm not sure if she did it on purpose, but Isabelle has found a solution to my time management problem. Although it's still March and far from warm, there's no risk of rain today—hardly a cloud in the clear, blue winter sky!—and a stroll through the city while we wait for the restaurants to open might be exactly what we need.

"The promenade by the Garonne is really nice, though. Have you been there lately?" I nod in direction of the river, at the other side of the city center. On foot, it will take us at least thirty minutes to get there.

Isabelle lights up. "I haven't, not since I got home. Guess I didn't think of going there when it's cold." Both sides of the river are very popular places to hang out on sunny summer day but attempting the same in winter can be a cold experience.

I'm a fraction of a second from saying I'll keep her warm. "As long as we keep moving, we should be fine. And the area around Place Saint-Pierre has a lot of excellent restaurants. If you were serious about that?" I trail off, doubts assailing me again.

Isabelle's gaze meets mine and her beautiful smile goes a long way toward removing my worries. "As long as you don't turn into a jerk again, I'd love to have dinner with you." She bites her lip as her eyes turn distant. "Someplace with proper duck, please. The English don't know how to cook."

"Everybody knows the English don't have proper food. I can't believe you willingly moved there." We start walking down the wide avenue, close but not quite touching at the shoulders. I want to reach out and grab her gloved hand but that turns out to be beyond the reach of my limited courage. Instead, I let my hand swing rather than shove it in my pockets like I usually do—just in case Isabelle is more courageous than me.

We continue discussing food and cultural differences until we reach the maze of narrow streets that make up the historical center of Toulouse. Hardly any right angles and no landmarks that stand out above the others, I've had to help many a hapless tourist find their way.

Since Isabelle seems to ooh and aah at every food specialty shop we go by, I adapt our trajectory to include my favorite *fromager*—I manage to talk Isabelle out of buying a blue cheese capable of walking out of the shop on its own only because she agrees it won't like spending so much time in the relative heat of the restaurant and she promises the owner she'll be back tomorrow—and two of my favorite *chocolatiers*. For once, I anticipate somewhat, and buy us a small collection of chocolates to share, asking Isabelle to choose the flavors.

We stop in one of the side streets off rue Saint-Rome, more of an alley really, to dig into our purchase. Isabelle chooses a dark chocolate with raspberry filling and I opt for the one with coffee liqueur. We touch the pieces together in a toast and bite down.

I shove the whole piece into my mouth—it's not even the size of my thumb, why wouldn't I—and the mix of chocolate, alcohol, and coffee flood my senses. The ganache inside the chocolate melts on my tongue and I let out a small moan.

Which turns into a groan when Isabelle daintily bites of half of her sweet, her red lips sliding over the chocolate and her fingers, and her eyes closing in bliss.

I realize I'm close enough to smell the raspberry. I even catch a whiff of her rosy shampoo. I've crowded her up against the brick wall and I'm not sure I have the strength to step away.

Popping the rest of her chocolate into her mouth, Isabelle opens her eyes and looks right into mine. And smiles. "It's so good." When I can't get out a single word, only stare at her lips and into her eyes, she adds in a whisper, "Wanna taste?"

That's all the invitation I need. I lean in the remaining inch and close my lips over hers.

The best taste in the world? A heady mix of dark chocolate, raspberry, alcohol, coffee, and Isabelle.

THIRTY-SIX

Excellent Choice of Chocolate

Isabelle

I'M THE ONE who asked Thomas to have dinner with me tonight, but a lingering doubt of whether or not it was a good idea stayed with me. As long as I'm living in the moment, I'm enjoying myself, thrilled at spending some time alone with Thomas, walking the streets of Toulouse. But then a man's profile will remind me of Pierre, and I wonder if Thomas really is different or if he's just putting on a show and the real him will come out later. Too late.

Or I'll see a travel agency and remember I don't have a job here yet, and can't guarantee I'll find one, and starting something with Thomas might be a bad idea. Will I be able to leave him if I get an offer for a position I want in a different city?

I need to make it on my own, but that doesn't necessarily mean I have to *be* alone.

All of this goes through my mind while we wander through the streets of Toulouse, window-shopping and chatting. But for every time Thomas makes me laugh, or points out a shop he thinks I'll like, or looks as unsure as I'm feeling, I move one step closer to wanting to give this a try with him.

If I don't, I'll regret it. *That* is a certainty.

I might not have been single and looking for someone for fifteen years, but I still had eyes. And the number of guys I could envision myself with isn't all that high. Don't I owe it to myself, and my happiness, to give it a shot when I find someone who makes my heart thump so loudly?

Instead of running from my past mistakes, I can learn from them, and make sure I don't step on the same land mines.

When Thomas steps closer while we taste our delicious chocolate, I don't feel threatened or crowded. I feel wanted.

So I invite him in.

The kiss will be forever branded into my mind. The contrast between the cold hard brick wall in my back and the soft warmth of Thomas against my front. The coffee and raspberry flavors of our two chocolates mixing as the kiss deepens. And the light scratch of Thomas's stubble as our lips move together.

My hands slide into his hair. His go to my waist and against my chin.

The clack-clack-clack of an old bike rolling past on the paving stones barely registers. I feel *wanted* for the first time in so long, I think I'd forgotten what it felt like. If I'd remembered, I might have left Pierre years earlier.

I'm not sure how long we stand there, making out like teenagers, exploring what we can through the thick winter clothing. We're brought back to reality when three girls come chatting down the alley and start giggling so hard when they spot us, it almost sounds painful.

Thomas pulls back so there's some space between us but close enough I can still feel the heat of his body against mine. I'd feel embarrassed by the goofy smile I'm giving him, except he's doing the exact same thing, and my insides melt even further.

"Excellent choice of chocolate," Thomas says. He presses a thumb to the corner of my mouth, removing a stray dab of chocolate. "We should do that more often."

"Excellent idea. In fact…" I'm surprised to find what I say next isn't scary at all. It feels exactly right. "I think I've ruined my appetite with that *chocolatine* earlier and these sweets now. It would be a shame to order a big meal in a restaurant and not eat everything. How about we do a rain check for the restaurant and bring something simple to eat at your place instead?"

It's a little odd to invite myself to his place, but I live with my parents. We're *not* going there.

Thomas's eyes darken and he hovers closer. I'd hardly need to move at all for our lips to touch again. "I have a box of duck confit at home. Leftovers from the holidays but it should still be good. The rest of our chocolate for dessert?"

"That sounds perfect." I figure there's no point in depriving myself, and lean up for a quick kiss. Which evolves into a long kiss. When the big clothing gets too annoying, I pull away. "What's the quickest route to get to your place?"

Breathing hard, Thomas grabs my hand and pulls me toward the rue Saint-Rome. "Metro. This way."

I don't think we'll be having the duck tonight.

But the dessert and its inevitable consequences will be delicious.

EPILOGUE

Ten months later

Thomas

THE FASTEN SEATBELT sign switches on as we emerge from the layer of clouds and the low February sun shines through the window to blind me. A baby is crying three seats back and a man in his fifties has been negotiating for a bottle of whiskey with the hostess for five minutes already. My bets are on a no. I don't bother closing the blinds—we haven't seen the sun in a month in Toulouse and I'll take what I can get.

Besides, Isabelle is sleeping in the window seat and I don't want to wake her.

We got up at four this morning, so we could be at the airport in time for a six o'clock flight. Vincent drove us in his old wreck of a car, bouncing red pom-pom the only indication he was awake behind the wheel. We had a stopover in Amsterdam which was supposed to be two hours long, but was shortened to fifty minutes because someone didn't show up to the gate in Toulouse and they had to find and remove his luggage from the hold.

I couldn't stop grinning as we sprinted through Schiphol Airport, zig-zagging between other travelers and risking limbs with our bouncing carry-ons. I wasn't happy about potentially missing our flight to Athens, nor about our dwindling chances of arriving with all our bags, but it brought back memories of the day we first met.

And the similarities continued as Isabelle fell asleep the minute we found our seats. She never does handle having her usual morning routine messed with.

I can learn from past mistakes, though. I let her have the window seat. I'll be getting up to use the lavatory in a minute, and I won't even run the risk of getting punched. Not that I think Isabelle would reflexively throw a punch today.

Therapy has done its thing, as has time and closure in the form of official divorce papers. She's much more at ease today than the day we met, allowing her to be her awesome, fascinating self.

Isabelle planned our three-day weekend trip to Athens, of course. She's working part time for a travel agency in the historical center of Toulouse and spends the rest of her time as a consultant for companies like my own, who produce IT products touching on travel, history, or art. When going to a place like Athens, the difficulty wasn't in finding things to see, but deciding on which things *not* to see. And figuring out an itinerary with elements that will interest the both of us. Not too simple for her, not too detailed for me.

As long as I get to spend three days and nights with my girl, I'm happy. But she wanted to set up the perfect itinerary, so I let her.

And Saturday is Valentine's Day. My hand touches on the box in my jeans' pocket, making sure it's still there. I've made the reservations for dinner on Saturday—the nicest place I could find close to our hotel—and even paid extra for the most romantic seat in the house, to make sure everything is perfect.

Isabelle moved into my apartment two months ago. She had her own place, but when a second plant died because of lack of water and light since she was never there, we decided we might as well make it official. Her mother frowned when we gave her the news but she tends to do that with everything.

I want to make it even more official. I may also have been cheered on by my colleagues since they heard about our plans for this weekend. One of the guys asked—as a joke—if I was proposing and I answered I was thinking about it. They've all been telling me to go for it ever since. Anita in her very direct way, telling me there's no way Isabelle will say no and if I don't do it, she will. The guys by finding pictures of the worst engagement rings in the world and betting on which will be the closest to the one I choose.

In my bag, I have a second ring, the worst I could find for less than five euros. The plan is to get Isabelle to wear it for a picture and see if the guys at work buy it.

The lady from across the aisle comes back from the lavatory and I release my belt to go back there myself. But before I get up: I lean over to where Isabelle is propped up against the window and kiss her on the cheek.

She smiles, sighs in contentment, and goes back to sleep.

Author's Note

THANK YOU FOR reading *Love at First Flight*. Originally, it was supposed to be a short story. Except it wasn't. Getting my protagonists together after four or five chapters felt way too rushed for these two, so I figured I'd give them an entire novel.

And I didn't regret it for a second.

It certainly allowed me to zone out from the outside world for a bit (yes, this was written during the pandemic) and I hope it has allowed you some escape, too. If you did enjoy it, feel free to leave an honest review on your favorite platform so other readers can discover it.

If you want to stay updated on any new stories, I invite you to sign up for my newsletter on rwwallace.com. You can opt in or out of the genres you're interested in, so you can get updates only on romance books for example, or add in mystery... You can even choose to get information (in French) about French translations!

R.W. Wallace
rwwallace.com

Also by R.W. Wallace

Romance

French Office Romance Series
Flirting in Plain Sight
Hiding in Plain Sight
Loving in Plain Sight
(tie-in short story, available through newsletter)

Mystery

Ghost Detective Novels
Beyond the Grave
Unveiling the Past
Beneath the Surface

Ghost Detective Shorts
Just Desserts
Lost Friends
Family Bonds
Common Ground
Till Death
Family History
Heritage
Eternal Bond
New Beginnings
Severed Ties

Ghost Detective Collections
Unfinished Business, Vol 1

The Tolosa Mystery Series
The Red Brick Haze
The Red Brick Cellars
The Red Brick Basilica

Short Story Collections
Deep Dark Secrets
A Thief in the Night

Holiday Short Stories
Down the Memory Aisle
Morbier Impossible
A Second Chance
The Magic of Sharing
The Case of the Disappearing Gingerbread City
The Lucia Crown
Crooks and Nannies

Time Travel Secrets (short stories)
Moneyline Secrets
Family Secrets

Young Adult Short Story Collections
Tales From the Trenches

Find all R.W. Wallace's books:

rwwallace.com/allbooks

About the Author

R.W. WALLACE WRITES in most genres, though she tends to end up in mystery more often than not. Dead bodies keep popping up all over the place whenever she sits down in front of her keyboard. Except when a romance just *has* to come out. Or when a whole new fantasy world is taking form in her mind... You get the point.

The stories mostly take place in Norway or France; the country she was born in and the one that has been her home for two decades. Don't ask her why she writes in English—she won't have a sensible answer for you.

Her Ghost Detective short story series appears in *Pulphouse Magazine*, starting in issue #9.

You can find all her books, long and short, all genres, on her website: rwwallace.com.

www.ingramcontent.com/pod-product-compliance
Lightning Source LLC
LaVergne TN
LVHW032005070526
838202LV00058B/6297